ONE

Two shots and then a third echoed from the saloon. The Indian lounging opposite the saloon, near a hitching rail, went into action. Swiftly he unloosed the row of horses and waited. From the corner of his eye, he saw the black man, Joshua, turn and watch the sheriff's office from the corner from where he was standing.

The few townsfolk on the street froze and then scattered into doorways. Then, without warning, the batwing doors burst open. Two men spilled out and one, looking back, fired a warning shot into the wooden ceiling. The other man, tall, young and lanky, laughed and then both sprang for their horses.

The Indian was already astride and struggling with the rest of the startled horses. Joshua, now grinning, loped across the road just as the sheriff and his deputies erupted from his office jail.

'What the hell . . ?' he bawled, but took one look at the Indian, the black man and the two white

5

men, now mounting up, and the weapons they carried, turned with a curse and ushered his men back inside the jail.

'It's the Wilde mob! Better keep your heads down, boys. What they're doing in town is none of our business! God curse the sons of bitches!'

Outside, the men held their horses in check, their eyes on the window above the saloon. Suddenly there came another two shots and the sash of the window was flung up and a figure scrambled out and ran with crouching gait along the balcony. He paused and looked back as a woman appeared at the window, her white lacy basque splattered with blood.

She poked her head out of the window and raised her fist at the man.

'God damn you, Sabre Wilde, for a mad dog murderer! You nearly killed me, too! Now I'll have to change the sheets!'

Sabre Wilde laughed and put his fingers to his lips and blew her a kiss.

'Sorry, Alice; if you sleep with skunks, you come to smell like 'em. Someday I'll be back and I'll make it up to you. I promise!'

'Like hell you will! You've cut off my main source of income. I hope you rot in Hell!' But Alice Lovejoy's lips puckered in a reluctant smile. Rumour had it that Sabre Wilde was good in bed and respected a woman's feelings, even though he was the most unpredictable outlaw in the West.

She watched as he sprang down lightly into the

The Outcasts

JAMES O. LOWES

A Black Horse Western

ROBERT HALE · LONDON

© James O. Lowes 1998
First published in Great Britain 1998

ISBN 0 7090 6245 1

Robert Hale Limited
Clerkenwell House
Clerkenwell Green
London EC1R 0HT

*For my sons and daughter
who have loved and supported me
during the highs and lows of my life.
Thank you.*

Photoset in North Wales by
Derek Doyle & Associates, Mold, Flintshire.
Printed bound in Great Britain by
WBC Book Manufacturers Limited, Bridgend.

To John & Carol,

All my Love!
James C Lowes

_____

July '98

The Outcasts

By the same author

Lawful Assassins

bed of a wagon half loaded with sacks of flour, and then to the ground. Then he grabbed the reins of his horse that the Indian held ready, raked its sides and thundered out of town with his men following behind. She turned and surveyed the dead man in her bed and the splatter of blood and shook her head.

On the outskirts of town, an old, bald-headed man waited. He was Bill Roscoe, one-time sergeant in the Union Army. It was his job to guard the pack horses, for they had a long way to go, and spurned the townships and lived off the land – voluntary outcasts, doing the dirty jobs for a president who couldn't be seen doing them for himself.

Major Horatio Wilde, known as Sabre Wilde, the outlaw, and his loyal troop of men, neither in the army nor out of it, were destined to do their duty no matter how distasteful.

Outside the small township, Sabre Wilde pulled his horse to a walk, took out a list and crossed off two names – Colonel John Buchan and Elijah Swindley, the first a one-time officer in the Union Army who had organized and commanded his own regiment, and the second who had owned a gun-running ship and, with the colonel's help, had made a fortune for them both.

The colonel had become a senator and the owner of a chain of saloons while Swindley had become a banker and a respectable member of the church in the new town named after him called

Swindley Crossing just off the Chisholm Trail.

Now both were defunct by order of the President of the United States.

Sabre Wilde's bleak glance took in the silent watching men. All showed signs of strain, except perhaps young Skinner who just obeyed orders and considered what they were doing was just a prolonged act of war. Traitors had to be sought out and summarily dealt with and all the names on Sabre Wilde's list were men of violence who deserved to die. So, what the hell? Do the job and forget it and enjoy the respite between strikes.

'Right, boys, any comments?' Wilde looked keenly at them all. Ned Skinner coughed but said nothing. He was the youngest and of lowest rank; nobody took note of him. He was only thankful he wasn't responsible for the outcome of these sorties.

George Lucas, captain under Major Horatio Wilde before their lives had been turned upside down by order of President Johnson, coughed and spat in the dust.

'I want to report Skinner, here. His target was the saloon pay-roll while I despatched Swindley while you sought out Buchan.'

Sabre Wilde nodded. 'Yes? That's what happened, didn't it?' He looked at Skinner. 'You got the pay-roll?'

Ned Skinner nodded and held up a leather bag and tossed it to Wilde.

George Lucas flushed with anger.

'But that wasn't the end of it. He brought down two cowboys: one of them wounded, the other killed. The orders specifically stated that there was to be no excess killing. I say that was wanton murder and . . .'

'That's a lie! It wasn't murder!' Ned cast a resentful glance at Lucas and his right hand went to his hip. Old Bill Roscoe leaned over and caught his wrist.

'Not so fast, son. Don't do anything you'll be sorry for.'

Ned pulled his wrist free. 'It's a lie! It wasn't wanton! It was necessary. The man I shot was a professional gunman and he was aiming at the captain's back. I saved his life! The other . . . he got between me and the safe. You wanted the payroll, you got it.' He looked sullenly at the man he worshipped above all others. Sabre Wilde wasn't only his superior officer but his family as well. For Ned, at twenty-two, had no other family. If he had not volunteered to follow Major Wilde along the owlhoot trail after the war, he would have become a drifter and perhaps have succumbed to his wild temper, for Ned was impulsive, unpredictable and headstrong.

He was the weak link in the chain that was the small tight-knit unit operating as an outlaw gang to bring justice to the traitors to the Government of the United States of America.

They were no ordinary traitors. These men on the president's list were men in high places with influence. They had to be disposed of quietly and discreetly, for public disclosure could bring down the government.

There were also Rebels to be taken care of; men responsible for torturing prisoners, for allowing the violation of women and the looting of homes and who now considered themselves safe because the war was over.

For them it was a fool's paradise, for the hatreds and the atrocities on both sides would never be forgotten and Nemesis was slowly, but surely, tracking them down. . . .

Sabre Wilde studied Ned Skinner. Old Bill could control him. He had taken the place of Ned's father and the boy listened when Bill gave him a fatherly lecture. He saw how the boy was calming down under Bill's influence and turned to George Lucas.

'I think you should retract your words, George. The boy saved your life.'

George Lucas grunted and jerked his horse's bridle, pulling back his head.

'What are we waiting for?' He dug his spurs into the horse's ribs and rode savagely ahead.

The Apache ex-scout, Johnny Eagle Eye, also known as Johnny Bronco, and the freed slave, Joshua, who'd been silent onlookers during the exchange, looked at each other. Joshua murmured softly, 'There sure goes one hell of an angry man!'

Sabre Wilde heard the remark but ignored it. He raised his arm and waved them on.

'Come on, boys, let's ride. We have a long way to go before sunset!'

But his heart was heavy. He could see trouble ahead between George Lucas and Skinner, trouble that could easily be the downfall of them all!

TWO

Big Mal Buchan gave a bellow of rage and crushed the telegraph message in his hand. The little man from the telegraph office cringed as Mal Buchan's fist came up to strike.

'I'm sorry, Mr Buchan, sir,' he gulped. 'I'm only bringing what came over the wire!'

Mal Buchan breathed deeply, suddenly aware that reaction to the news had made him lash out at little crippled Tom Baines, whose only misdemeanour was to urinate on the sidewalk on a Saturday night when he'd had a skinful . . . a minor offence when one thought of the murders, rapes and lesser sundry evils of cold-cockings, robberies and stabbings he had to attend to. He grunted.

'Aw, not your fault, Tom. You're only doing your duty.' Then he slammed one meaty fist into the palm of the other hand. 'But, by God, I'll get that bastard and his turncoat gang if it means turning in my badge. I'll get them!'

Tom Baines watched him curiously – at a distance. He didn't trust Big Mal's temper. He was the most ruthless marshal Abilene's townsfolk had known in years and he was the most hated.

Inside, the little man was laughing, not because Big Mal's brother had been mown down in one of his own saloons, but because Big Mal now knew what it was like to lose a member of his family.

Big Mal was an arrogant bastard, standing six feet four and broad with it, with a kick like a mule and a punch like a sledgehammer and reflexes that were one jump ahead of any gun-happy cowboy looking for trouble.

The trouble was he was too good, a mean, trigger-happy, short-fused madman, who seemed obssessed with filling up Boothill as fast as humanly possible. Some of the stiffs carted up there and planted quick, had certainly not deserved such short shrift.

The townsfolk grumbled to each other but kept their murmurings low. It didn't pay to make an enemy of Big Mal; his deputies had a nasty habit of falsifying evidence. Anyone who could, paid a hefty fine to get out of jail, or else they were left languishing and living on grub supplied by the worst cook in town.

Big Mal had walked the main street of Abilene many times, declaring he didn't give a shit for the bereaved families of those he'd gunned down. If they didn't like it, they could face him, eye to eye, or leave town. It was their choice.

Tom Baines couldn't wait to twang the grapevine and let the town know that Big Mal Buchan's brother had been shot and killed by Sabre Wilde or one of his gang. It was Hallelujah Day!

Big Mal swung round on his heel and pointed a hard hand at Tom.

'And you, you miserable little creep, a whisper about this and I hear of it and, by God, I'll tear your balls off by hand! Understand me?'

Tom nodded until he thought his head would drop off. 'Yessir! Yessir! I get you! Not a word, sir. I would never . . .'

'Oh, yes you would if you dared! I've heard those murmurings in the saloons on Saturday nights when tongues speak loud and loose! I've got a list of names and, by God, if you let slip about this here message, I'll put your name on top of it! You'll have to live watching your back in future. You understand?'

Tom choked back the hate bile in his mouth.

'Yes, sir. You can rely on me.' He tried a laugh, but it came out as a groan. 'You really don't think I'd talk? Why, I'm one of your most loyal supporters!'

Big Mal gave him a hard glance and spat on the dirt floor.

'Get to hell outa here!' Tom got.

Big Mal smoothed out the telegram again and read the message. He cursed and slammed his desk. This time he wasn't thinking about John. He was thinking about the chain of saloons and the woman who'd shared John's bed. She called herself Alice Lovejoy. Big Mal would have bet his last dollar that Lovejoy wasn't her real name, but it was effective all right! He detested her, for hadn't she been creaming off the profits of the saloons when half should have come to him as his brother? But when Mal had offered to go into partnership when he saw John was striking gold, his brother had laughed and said Alice was the only partner he needed.

Yet Alice's name always raised a reaction in Mal. He hated her for it.

Now he was determined to go after Sabre Wilde and his gang of ex-army cutthroats, get the kudos for ridding the West of the scourge and, after that, maybe taking John's place in the senate and certainly taking over the saloons and Alice Lovejoy . . . well, it would depend on how co-operative she was. One way or another Alice would get her comeuppance.

But first there was the matter of going on leave. He would have to square it with the governor who would send in another marshal to Abilene. Two of the deputies he'd take with him, hard men who welcomed a scrap, and he'd pick up a few of the town scroungers who were good with guns, men who thrived on quick sharp sorties but couldn't stand permanent work. He knew just the right men for the job in hand. He could afford good wages; after all, he would come in for John's stash and the men had the lure of gunning down the most dangerous outlaw gang in the territories. That would bring 'em! He smiled. He was looking forward to this. Life had been dull lately. It was time he was back on the road, feeling the wind in his hair and the smell of sage in his nostrils again.

He must send out a message to all counties and find out where Sabre Wilde had been sighted since the raid at Swindley Crossing. He pinned up a map of the territory and stuck a pin into the dot that was Swindley Crossing and then drew a circle around it. His eyes narrowed as he noted the towns nearest to the ring. He would send his messages to the sheriffs and marshals concerned. Soon, he would be ready to ride.

The camp-fire was burning low, the wood ash turning from red to pinkish grey. A smoke-blackened coffee-pot stood nearby, half full of stewed coffee for the use of the man on watch through the first part of the night. A stick collapsed and, for a moment, a tongue of flame leapt upwards and then died away. A recumbent figure stirred and snorted and pulled a dark-grey blanket further about his shoulders. He slept on.

Ned Skinner's head drooped and then came upright. He looked around, but saw nothing. He decided the noise that had awakened him must have come from the fire. He got up from his haunches and stepped closer and threw on a few more sticks. Soon there was more smoke and small flames licked the branches and the coffee-pot started to sizzle.

He took his kerchief and lifted the pot and poured some of the strong brew into a battered mug and drank. It burnt his lips and he cursed quietly so as not to awaken the sleeping men.

A new moon shone fitfully behind drifting clouds. It had the appearance of rain to come. Ned shivered. He hoped they would reach Allens Butte before the storm broke. At this time of year a storm could last for days. Allens Butte meant a soft bed and maybe a willing female and as much drink as he could stomach. The boss always allowed them to let their hair down after one of their sorties.

He smiled wryly. The major considered a successful termination, as he called it, something to celebrate. The captain now, he thought differently. A queer bastard, the captain. Sometimes a feller couldn't decide which side he was on. After all, they was all soldiers and soldiers killed, didn't they? Nobody thought anything about it in wartime. And this was still wartime, wasn't it, as long as there were traitors out there to be caught and shot? Anyhow, the major said it was the right thing to do. The president himself had given them orders, so they couldn't be murderers in the proper sense of the word.

Ned often talked to himself when Bill wasn't around to listen to his reasoning. Anyhow, Bill got humpy sometimes as if he, too, had misgivings, but he would never hear a word against the major and if it came to push against shove he'd back the major against the captain any time. As for the mischief-making captain, he didn't give a damn about him. He wished he'd never seen that gunman aim for Lucas's back . . . he was the one who stirred up trouble amongst them. Yet the major let him have his say. Ned couldn't understand it.

He emptied the coffee dregs and stood up and stretched. Time for a walk around and check the horses before awakening Joshua.

Quietly he moved away from the fire and before seeing to the horses, urinated against a tree. There was a rustle in the trees as a startled bird flew upwards. Ned cursed under his breath and moved on. The horses stood quietly sleeping, tethered to a long rope. Moving lightly, he inspected the several packs that had not been opened. All were intact, nothing disturbed.

He was turning to walk back to camp to awaken Joshua when his attention was caught by a dark mound that moved ever so softly. What the hell?

He squatted down and peered into the half shadows and felt the warmth of a blanket. In one single movement, he snatched back the blanket and pulled his gun and found he was looking down at the thin, white face of a girl who looked up at him with frightened eyes.

'Don't shoot!' she begged. 'I'll come back with you quietly if you don't shoot. I'm sorry I ran away. . . .' Then she stopped and peered closer. 'You're not Zaracov. Who are you?'

'I might say the same to you, miss. Who are you?'

'I'm . . . I'm . . . it doesn't matter who I am. I'm not doing any harm. Please just forget about me. I'll be gone in the morning.'

'And where the hell would you go with no horse? It's desert that way and forest back over. How would you survive? I think you'd better come and see our boss.'

'*No!* Please! Just let me go! I promise not to bother you again.' She tried to wriggle away from him and managed to scrabble to her knees, but he grabbed her by her hair and she turned to claw and fight him.

The row awakened the camp and old Bill, looking like a ghost in just his dirty grey long-johns and vest hobbled over, his grey hair about his ears, unkempt and straggly.

'What's going on, Ned? You've got the horses jumping and ready to bust their rope.' He stopped suddenly and gawked at what Ned was holding well away from flailing fists. 'I see you've caught yourself a wildcat!' he guffawed and grabbed the girl's wrists. 'Come on now, m'beauty, let's have a look at you.' He and Ned led her struggling into the faint light from the camp-fire.

The men were now all awake and stared at the

captive as Sabre Wilde stood up and came towards them.

'Well . . . well! Now here's a pretty sight! Just what is a little lady like you doing out here in the wilds all on your ownsome?'

She was thin, a little package not more than five feet five, with no breasts to speak of, but she made up for it in sheer grit and whiplash strength. She wore a torn black skirt and a man's check shirt which somehow made her delicately boned face all the more feminine. But it was her long, glossy black hair that fascinated them all. It fell like a silky curtain nearly to her narrow boyish behind.

She was a beauty all right, and maybe not more than eighteen years old.

'What's your name, child?'

She glared at Sabre Wilde.

'I'm not a child! At least Ivan Zaracov didn't treat me as a child!' Sabre Wilde's head jerked up and his eyes narrowed. He'd heard that name before. He bowed.

'Then I must apologize. I am Sabre Wilde and these are my good friends. Now, who are you?' He gestured to Ned to free her and he did so. She snatched her hand away and massaged her wrist, glaring at him.

She was like a young vixen at bay, surrounded by would-be hunters. But she was defiant. She flung back her head, her blue-black hair a wild curtain about her.

'I'm Carla Juarez,' she answered sullenly.

'And what are you doing out here all alone? And why didn't you come into camp?

She gave a hard laugh. 'And risk being subjected to attack? I'd just escaped from Zaracov, and I wanted to observe you all in the light of day.'

'And if you didn't like what you saw?'

'Then I should have tried to steal some food and been on my way!'

'You're hungry! Joshua, rustle up some grub for the lady. Ned, pour her some coffee.'

It was when Carla smelled the coffee that she suddenly wilted and sank to her knees. Sabre Wilde scooped her up in his arms and carried her to the camp-fire and sat her down on his blanket.

She ate ravenously, like a young savage, choking on the cold chilli and hunk of bread. Finally, after a second mug of coffee, she sat back and belched and then, smiling for the first time, sighed with satisfaction.

'I'm sorry I was rude. I was frightened. I thought you would be like Zaracov.'

'Ah, yes, Zaracov. Tell me about him.' Sabre sat closer to her.

She looked around at the other men who were now settling down again to sleep. Their actions calmed her fears. There would be no assault on her person this night. She looked at Sabre Wilde in the flickering firelight and though the livid scar on his face had first startled her, she saw that the hawk face could be trusted. His eyes also told her that he was interested in Zaracov rather than herself.

The thought of Zaracov made her eyes gleam and her lips curled back from her teeth like an enraged animal.

'Zaracov! I swear that some day I'll kill him!' She beat the ground with her fists. 'He's a devil! He killed my father and my mother. He's a mud-crawling dung beetle! I hope he rots in Hell!' Suddenly she was sobbing and Sabre put an arm about her and she buried her face into his chest.

He let her cry and, when the wave of despair and anger had lessened, he said softly, 'Tell me about him. How did your parents get mixed up with him?' She sniffed and hiccuped and blew her nose on the hem of her skirt.

Sabre gestured to George Lucas who was sitting close by and George produced a bottle of whiskey. He handed it to Carla who hesitated and then took a drink. She coughed, but it brought colour to her cheeks and she was able to talk with a controlled calm that spoke volumes.

'We had a *ranchero* on the border of New Mexico. We saw few people as it was in the mountains. The nearest village was half a day's ride and sometimes we didn't see strangers for weeks. One day my father was driving back from the village with dry goods from the store. He was singing, for he was a little drunk you understand, having been to the *taverna*. He came upon a wounded man, shot in the shoulder. His horse was standing by, grazing. It looked as if it had been ridden hard. My father, being drunk, was not wary. He loaded the man into the wagon, caught the horse and tied it to the wagon and he brought him home to us.' She paused, breathing deeply, remembering the sensation it had caused bringing a strange man into their home.

'And how long did he stay?'

'It was three days before he woke up. I was sitting by him when he opened his eyes. At first he spoke in a strange language that afterwards I realized was Russian. But later on he spoke English with an accent. He told us that his mother was Irish and his father a trapper from way up in Alaska. His father had left his mother when he was a baby and came back when he was ten or eleven years old. His mother had died and he'd gone back to Russia with his father. A lot of this had come out during his delirium and my mother had listened and remembered and told my father and myself. She thought it was like an adventure story.'

'Then what happened?'

'When he got stronger and found out we knew so much, he changed. He got angry and accused us of spying on him. He attacked my father and chained him up in our storehouse. Then he threatened my mother and said he would kill both my father and me if she did not cook for him and sleep with him.'

'And what did you do?'

'I went for him with a knife and he locked me up in my bedroom so that I did not know what was happening. Then the men came.'

'The men?'

'Yes. Two men came riding into our yard. He came into my room and looked out of the window and when he pulled the curtain back, I saw them. He cursed both in Russian and English and I asked him who they were. He said they were Pinkerton men, whoever they were. I'd never heard of them before. He laughed and said they weren't the first who'd been on his trail, but he always outwitted the stupid idiots. Then he broke the window and aimed his rifle and one of them fell off his horse.'

'And what about the other man?'

'He ran and hid behind the barn. The firing went on all day, then my mother opened the door and ran out and he shot her in the back. . . .' Carla's hands went up to her mouth as she relived the sight of her mother sprawling in the dust and the growing scarlet stain on her back.

'Then one time when the man fired at him, he let out a loud scream and didn't fire back and after a while the man came looking for him and that was when Zaracov shot him between the eyes.'

'What happened then?'

'He was in a hurry to get away. He said that if they could find him, others would follow. He bundled up some food and all the tequila he could find into the cart and tied his horse to it. Then he forced me into the cart with him. He said it was a shame to leave me behind and he tied my wrists to one of the shafts while he went back to the house. I called after him, 'What of my father?' and he turned and laughed.

'That was when he killed him?'

'Oh, he didn't kill him. He left him to burn in the barn, tied to a manger. He fired the house and the wind caught the barn and the dry hay and straw burned easily. I screamed and screamed and finally he hit me and when I awakened, I was lying in the bottom of the wagon miles away from my home.'

Sabre's face had set grimly as he listened. During one of the secret meetings with the president's envoy, Zaracov's name had cropped up. He wasn't on Sabre Wilde's list for he was being hunted by Pinkerton's men and the United States marshal's agents. But it had been requested that if he was sighted, the agency had to be notified.

Ivan Zaracov was one of Russia's most wanted spies, who'd caused unrest up in Alaska because of the purchase of Alaska from Russia for more than $7 million, thus ruining the Russian fur trade. There were dissenters on both sides who were against the purchase and Zaracov had blazed a trail of murder and political intrigue for his masters in St Petersburg.

'And where is he now?'

'In Hell, I hope!'

He shook her. 'Carla, listen to me. I know about Zaracov. Where is he?'

She looked at him curiously. 'Just who are you? You're not just a band of drifting cowboys. How do you know about him?'

'That doesn't concern you. I've got to know. He's an enemy of the United States.'

'I don't care about that. I'm Mexican, but I sure care what happens to him! I knocked him out with a rock. He wasn't expecting it. He was drunk on tequila and after he'd had his way with me, he fell asleep and forgot to bind my wrists. So I took this rock and I lifted it above my head and wham! I hit him as hard as I could!' She lifted her skinny arms and brought them down sharply to show how she'd done it. Her teeth showed in a snarl. She was like one of those mountain cats defying a more powerful predator.

She started to cry again and Sabre's fingers bit into her shoulders as he shook her.

'Where is he? How far did you come? Answer me, girl.'

She sniffed and looked up at him.

'I ran through the bush until I couldn't put one foot in front of the other and I lay down under a tree and I must have slept, for it was dark when I awakened. Then I walked . . . and walked . . . and the moon came up and I could smell smoke and coffee and I hid and watched you all eat but I was too frightened to show myself. I thought. . . .'

'You thought we'd treat you like he did.' She nodded without speaking.

'You poor little devil' She sniffed some more and then wiped her eyes with the back of her hand.

'Can I have what's left of the chilli?'

'Go on, eat up. Bust yourself. Joshua, brew another pot of coffee, it's going to be a long night.'

George Lucas and Roscoe drew near.

'What are you going to do, boss?' asked Lucas.

'It's obvious, isn't it?' He looked across at a silent but watchful Johnny Eagle Eye. 'Johnny can backtrack to the camp-site and see what's happened. He can report back and then we can decide what to do. Zaracov is not officially our quarry. If she didn't kill him we can at least alert those who are hunting him. If he's still there unconscious, Johnny can bring him back to camp.'

Carla sprang to her feet and whirled about to glare at Johnny Eagle Eye.

'No! If you find him, kill him, or I will if you bring him back here! He shot my mother and he left my father to burn! I want him dead!'

'Easy now, girl. It's hours since you knocked him out. He could be far away now. Let's just wait and see, shall we?' Sabre nodded to Johnny Eagle Eye who slipped away into the trees and went and crouched down at the place where Ned had found her. The girl's trail was easy to follow, broken twigs and dislodged stones and grasses told their own tale.

At last Carla was more than replete; she was

uncomfortable. She stood up and prowled about the camp-fire while Sabre studied her. Lucas squatted down beside him, a mug of coffee in his hand.

'We got ourselves a problem, boss. What do we do with her? She could be trouble.' He motioned to Ned who was covertly watching her and even Roscoe and Joshua were watching her with interest.

'Well, we can't leave her behind and she's too far away from home. . . .'

'She hasn't got a home. Zaracov fired it, remember?'

'We'll just have to leave her at the first town we come across.'

'And then what? Leave her to the mercies of some fat old madam in a brothel, or some sonofabitch who'll treat her like a lump of meat?'

'She'd be wary of getting involved with a man after her experience.'

'She might have no option if she's hungry!' Lucas spat and stared ahead. 'She's too young to be left on her own.'

'What do you suggest then?' Sabre looked at him curiously. He knew all about George Lucas's fiancée marrying another man during the war and how it had affected him. Lucas shrugged.

'She could ride with us.'

'And get her in a pot of trouble if anything happens to us?'

Lucas looked at Sabre squarely.

'I could do with a woman. I'd look after her.'

Sabre laughed. 'You're not serious? I wouldn't touch that little hell-cat with a cattle prod! She could stick a knife between your ribs as soon as look at you!'

Lucas shrugged. 'The secret's in the handling. Those Mex women love passionately or they hate with all the fiery power of Hell behind them.'

'So you're an expert on Mex women?' Sabre said, remembering the cool, sedate young woman he'd been introduced to during one of their rare leaves during the war, whom the brash young captain had worshipped in those days.

'Not exactly,' Lucas said abruptly. 'But there were several Mex women amongst the camp-followers. You must remember them?'

'Aye. They were good cooks and laundresses and they were generally fat.'

'She's not fat and just look at that hair!'

Sabre shrugged. 'Well, it's your funeral. You can always ask her. It will be interesting to see how she reacts!'

With that, he yawned and lay down with his head on his saddle and put his hat over his eyes. Lucas took the hint and sat with his back against a tree, broodingly watching the girl as she prowled like a cat up and down . . . up and down.

At last she went and looked down at the sleeping Sabre and very quietly covered herself with part of his blanket, sharing his warmth. Sabre, rousing a little, felt her body at his back and, smiling, drifted back to sleep.

Lucas, restless and angry that she'd chosen the boss, turned on the hard ground and willed himself to sleep.

Meanwhile, Johnny Eagle Eye swiftly followed the girl's blundering trail. It was easy to follow as she'd not tried to cover her tracks. He found the place where she'd dropped down exhausted and slept. Then he followed her weaving, zigzag sign which told him how desperately tired she had become. He'd found the traces of black thread where she had blundered into thorn bushes and even a tuft of long black hair caught up on a low-hanging branch. The upturned stones and displaced grass told a story of blind panic and flight, until he'd come to the campsight, now deserted of man, horses and wagon. It was all there, the story of scuffle and rape. Kneeling close to the dead camp-fire he found grey woollen fibres that had been torn from a blanket. He read the whole story and found the blood-spattered rock that had stunned the Russian.

He hadn't expected to find a dead body. A man wasn't killed so easily by a puny girl with a rock. He'd have one hell of a busting headache, but he'd live. Johnny found the wagon tracks leading away north. Maybe the white bastard was making for the tracks where the white man's iron horse ran smoothly. It was time to report to the boss.

THREE

The train ground to a halt with a great hiss of steam and a jolt. The grey-haired man in the faded denims and check shirt shouldered his worn saddle and hefted twin saddle-packs ready to alight. He took a swift look through the window; stockyards and more stockyards wherever he looked. That figured, he told himself. Abilene was the Mecca for all trail bosses. It would be one hell of a tough town.

He walked back along the track to the cattle trucks and unloaded his mare. His next stop would be the marshal's office which would be his own for the next few weeks or months as the case might be.

'Point me in the direction of the marshal's office.' His voice penetrated the fog of liquor surrounding a cowboy celebrating the end of a long haul up the Chisholm Trail.

'Eh, what's that, mister?'

'The marshal's office. Where is it?'

'Can't miss it. Follow your nose. Straight ahead.' The cowboy raised his bottle to his lips and drank and then let out a whoop of triumph. 'Yahoo!' Ben Dawson looked at him with pity and contempt.

'Thanks, mister, you're a big help!'

He forked his horse and rode down the straggly dirt track until he came to the shacks that were homes, saloons and stores. As the stranger had remarked, the marshal's office and jail stood out. They were of adobe and businesslike.

Stepping inside, he confronted the big man sitting at his desk with feet cocked up on the scarred surface.

'You Marshal Buchan? Mal Buchan?'

The marshal's feet dropped to the floor and his narrow gaze took in the tough-as-steel body, hard face and grey hair of the man before him.

'You be Ben Dawson, my replacement?'

'Yeh. Just why are you going after Sabre Wilde, Marshal? Don't you know he's the wiliest outlaw the West's seen in the last twenty years?'

Big Mal shrugged. 'Wily or not, I'm going to get him,' he answered gruffly. 'The man's a maniac. Shot my brother and his partner all out of the blue. No reason. He didn't even know them. Wanton murder it was.'

'There must have been a reason.'

'Nope! Just took the saloon takings. Not enough to murder two men for. Then they just rode out of town and the sheriff, God rot him, didn't even try to stop them!'

'It's happened before. The gang rides in, selects a target and before you can say hands up, they're gone, like phantoms in the wind. You know what they look like? I got some posters.'

'Good. I'll look 'em over. All I know is Wilde has a scarred cheek and there's an Apache and a black man riding with them. The others. . . .' He shook his head. 'They could be anybody.'

'Well, take your time. Better still, take them with you. Might come in handy. There's a good reward out for them. The governor's getting sick of hearing about them popping up. Some of his drinking buddies have come under his fire. He's a frightened man.'

Big Mal knew who to recruit. He wasted no time and left Ben Dawson to cope with his job, then headed past the OK Clothing Store, and Ham Bell's Livery stable and disappeared through the batwings of the Long Branch Saloon. There, he found four of the town's toughest gunnies arguing over a hand of poker and a fifth drinking at the bar. Red Gibson, an all-round wrestler, good with a knife as well as a gun: Pete Caine, a weasel of a man, quick with a knife and a good tracker; the two Macklyn brothers, Jock and Hamish, with good eyes for long-distance shooting and a devilish duo when it came to bar-room fighting; and the half-breed, Mitch Two Rivers, who would do anything for a bottle of rotgut whiskey. His party piece was to squeeze through any small hole or garrotte any man for a silver dollar.

Big Mal explained what was required and the reason for it. The Macklyn brothers pursed their lips.

'We've heard of the Wilde bunch. They're tricky. Shot a couple of Rebs we knew in the war. They had it coming. It was said they was spies and responsible for a lot of deaths. Yes sir! Maybe it was coincidence, I dunno. But they got away and didn't even stop to rob the bank where they were! It'll cost you, if we ride with you.'

'God dammit! I'm willing to pay! I'll pay you all good.'

They all grinned. All were in.

It was five days before Big Mal and his posse arrived in Swindley Crossing and learnt the details of the killing. But the trail was cold and it took time for Pete Caine to mingle amongst the townsfolk and listen and ask questions and deduce in what direction the gang had ridden. They visited the bank, interviewed the clerks, estimated the take and talked to the liveryman.

Then there were the witnesses and Big Mal visited his dead brother's saloon and interviewed a still shaken Alice Lovejoy.

'He burst in as bold as brass, wielding his gun at both of us. We were . . . er . . . still at it. John had no chance. I screamed and my legs got in the way of John leaping out of bed. We got tangled in the bedclothes, you know.' Alice gave Mal a wicked smile.

'I can guess,' Mal said tersely, 'but go on.'

Alice took a deep breath of indignation.

'The son of a bitch didn't even wait until I dived to the floor! He didn't care a damn about hitting me! I could have been the one shot to death in my own bed, God rot his black soul!'

'But you weren't. You're positive it was Wilde himself?'

'Oh, yes. He's a big man and would have been handsome if it wasn't for the scar on his cheek! They say he's good in bed. Not that he's been in my bed, you understand,' she said as Big Mal gave her a baleful glance. She smiled and sighed. 'I miss your brother. You remind me of him. You wouldn't. . . ?'

'No, I wouldn't.' He looked at the buxom flesh on the over-ripe Alice with distaste. His mind was on Sabre Wilde rather than on dallying in the bed where John had been shot. 'You can pack your bags and get out. This is my place now and I've got my own women coming in.'

'But you can't do that! I own half this place! I've been here for years!'

'And it shows,' he said brutally. 'I want some younger girls here to pep up the place. Last time I talked to John, he was grumbling about lack of trade. You're out!' He caught her wrist as she flew at him to punch him on the chin. He held her arm aloft as they faced each other eyeball to eyeball. 'I'll pay you out. I'll give you what I think you're worth.' Then he flung her from him.

She staggered back rubbing her wrist.

'You crawling slime worm! I hope Sabre Wilde gives you what you deserve, you lumbering bag of shit!'

His arm came up to strike her and she screamed. The bartender and the swamper came running. Both held shotguns trained on Big Mal.

'Leave her be, Mr Buchan. You might be John Buchan's brother but you're nothing to us here in Swindley Crossing.'

'This is my place now that my brother is dead and I'll tell you what to do! For a start, you two can get out. Bartenders are six a quarter.'

'Not so fast, mister. This here saloon belongs to Miss Alice and Elijah Swindley's son. John Buchan was a gambler. Get it?'

Mal Buchan cursed and then, without a word, turned on his heel and crashed out through the swing doors, Alice Lovejoy's raucous laughter following him.

Quickly he rounded up his men who were all taking advantage of the respite before the real hunt began. A blonde was draped around Red Gibson who was grinning like a lunatic because of where she had her hand. The Macklyn brothers were on the way to being drunk, while Mitch Two Rivers was well down a bottle of rotgut. Only Pete Caine appeared to be his usual self. He was a skinny man with delicate bones and a lugubrious expression and the swarthiness of an Italian. He was eating a huge plate of stew, for Pete was always hungry and yet he never put on flesh. He lived on his nerves.

He cocked his head in the direction of the half-breed, but did not stop shovelling stew into his mouth.

'You'd better talk to Mitch before he passes out. He's got on to the gang's trail. The old woman in the eatery said one of the gang let slip that they have a ranch in Arizona. She wasn't taking much notice of them. It was before the raid and to her they were just a bunch of cowboys passing through.'

'Well, I suppose that's something. I'll have a word with her.' Promptly, he took Mitch by the scruff of the neck and dragged him outside and dunked him in the horse trough.

He came up spluttering.

'What the hell did you do that for?'

'You should have come to seek me out when you found out which way they were headed!'

'You were busy with the whore. I didn't know what it might lead to,' Mitch protested. 'It wasn't as if an hour or so would make a difference!'

'It does now. We ride, pronto!'

'But. . . !'

'Look, dumbhead, I'm paying for results! They'll not head back for Arizona yet. We'll have to keep in touch with what's going on and that means keeping within distance of telegraph wires. If there is another raid, we can follow them until we come up with them. Understand?'

'Yeh, but that could be forever!'

'Forever or not. We follow. After all, they don't know we're on their trail. Sometime we're going to catch up and when we do . . .' – a look of vicious gloating crossed his face – 'he'll wish he'd never been born!'

When Pete gave his final belch and admitted he couldn't eat another mouthful, Big Mal herded them together and, though they grumbled, they followed him out of town before the sun had set. Alice Lovejoy watched them go, the bartender behind her.

'They'll be back,' she said almost absently. 'We haven't heard the last of that big fat bastard and when he does come back . . .' – she nodded at the bartender – 'we'll be ready for him. You keep the shotgun loaded, Charlie, and keep it handy!'

'I'll do that, Miss Alice. The nerve of him, to think he could come in and take over just like that! I'll have some of the boys keep a lookout for them. They'll not get far in this town again before all Hell will be popping!'

George Lucas watched the girl roll out of her blanket as dawn broke. The sun was coming up over the mountains with a glowing yellow-pink light. It was the time he liked best before the business of the day took over. But this morning he was in no mood to appreciate the freshness. He was eaten up with resentment that she'd chosen to bed down beside the boss.

No doubt she thought the older man was safer and more of a gentleman. She didn't know Sabre like he did. If she decided to ride with them she was certainly in for a surprise. He debated with himself when would be the best time to approach her with his proposition. By his reasoning, it was only common sense for her to make a commitment with one of them, then she would be protected at all times by her own man.

He glanced around at the others. Old Bill was already feeding the fire and the smell of coffee was wafting on the air. He and Sabre were the only ones not interested in watching the girl washing in the shallow stream that flowed with a rippling musical sound over water-smoothed stones.

She was a graceful sight and the shirt and trousers given by Lucas, only enhanced her femininity. By God, he would fight to have her! All memory of the pale girl who'd jilted him during the war, left him. This one was all fire and passion. You could see it in her eyes, and if he succeeded in her affections, then he would be a mighty lucky man, and his exile from family and friends bearable in the extreme.

For a while he watched and dreamed and then on impulse got up and followed her when she finally dried herself and walked away into the bushes. He waited until she emerged again and then, smiling, stopped her on the path.

'Could we talk?'

She looked at him with narrowed eyes. 'I want to eat. Is it important? I've told Sabre Wilde all he needs to know.'

'No. This is about your intentions. Do you still want to ride with us?'

'Yes, I made it clear last night. I'll not hold you back. I'm a good rider. I worked the farm with my father.' Her voice wobbled as she spoke his name and for a moment the pain showed in her eyes. 'I want to find Zaracov and the only way I can do that is to ride with you. You don't mind a woman riding with you? What about the others?'

Lucas shook his head.

'No one has objected, but I want to put a proposition to you. To be safe, you should belong . . . to one of us.' The last words came out in a rush. She stared hard at him and then began to laugh.

'You're joking, aren't you?' When he reddened and his face tightened at her laughter she frowned. 'You're not, are you? You really think that I could look at you all, make a snap decision and give myself to a man just so that he could protect me in a fight!'

'Well, why not? It would be better for us. That way there would be no fighting over you.'

'So it's for your convenience, is it?' Then her voice rose. 'I'm not a piece of meat, you know! I've got feelings and preferences and, right now, I don't need a man, thank you very much!'

'But it would make the situation simple. . . .' But before he could say any more she headbutted him in the chest and sent him sprawling.

'Another word, mister, and I'll scratch your goddamn eyes out!' She stormed back to the camp-fire where Bill was pouring coffee and dishing out thick rashers of pork belly on to hunks of bread.

Sabre watched her, interested in the outcome of Lucas's proposition. He had a hard time stifling a grin. Lucas joined him, a sulky look on his handsome face.

'Well? How did it go?'

Lucas cast him a dirty look. 'She didn't exactly think it was a good idea. But, by God, she's some woman! Zaracov was a fool!'

They were soon loaded up and ready to travel. Sabre gave her one more chance.

'D'you ride with us or do you want to stop off at the first town we come to?'

'I'll ride with you,' she answered with a determined air.

'I'm warning you now; we don't wait for stragglers. You keep up or you're on your own. Right?'

'Right!'

'You can ride one of the packhorses. We've got a spare saddle and you'll be responsible for feeding and cleaning your own horse. From now on you'll be treated as one of us. Understood?'

'Yes sir!'

'And you'll take orders without question?'

'Yes sir! That is if they're reasonable orders.'

'All orders. There might not be time to explain

the orders but when I say jump, you jump. Is that clear?'

She bit her lip and nodded.

'Right then. Let's ride. We've got a name to cross off our list and a rendezvous with a train on the night of the new moon!'

FOUR

The small group of men and the girl clustered together under the stand of trees. They watched the faint glow of light down in the valley. It came from a low sprawling ranchhouse surrounded by a number of buildings, one of which was a bunkhouse.

It was a rich man's spread. And no wonder, he thought, as Sabre mentally reviewed the top-secret file in his mind. Wilbur J. Hawkes, Colonel in the Confederate Army, a man known for his ferocity with his own slaves prior to joining the Rebels. A man who was soon to take command of one of the many prisoner-of-war camps around Richmond. Many Union soldiers had died because of his love of torture, others had died from starvation and the poor conditions in his camp. He had escaped during the assault by General Judson Kilpatrick in a bid to free the remaining prisoners. He was next heard of as a guerrilla commander, wreaking havoc on lonely homesteads and outposts to feed and sustain his band of men. Their loyalty to the cause had deteriorated to robbing and looting for their own benefit.

The general estimation was that Wilbur J. Hawkes was responsible for at least 10,000 deaths. He was now living on his own ranch under an assumed name. That name was Josiah B. Langford, a name he'd taken from a dead soldier during the rout engineered by General Kilpatrick in February 1864.

But the Pinkerton Agency had done its work well and now all that was left was the execution.

George Lucas stirred uneasily and his horse, conscious of his rider's nerves, whinnied and took several dancing steps.

'Quiet!' snapped Sabre. 'Nip his nostrils. Sound travels at night and there's sure to be a guard on duty.'

Lucas reached forward and muzzled his mount.

'I don't like it. This is just pure murder! We're not even giving him a chance!'

'You read the indictment. Did he give his victims a chance? How would you feel if he'd tortured your brother? Or violated your mother or sister? Name it, he's done it.'

'We've got no actual proof. Just the president's word and that of the army, and God knows I'm not sure I trust the military!'

Sabre Wilde looked at him with contempt and anger.

'We've had all this out before. If we can't trust

the president, who the hell can we trust? There are sworn affidavits from generals down to troopers. What more do you want?'

'I guess I'm squeamish when it's down to killing a man I don't have any quarrel with.'

'And giving him no warning. I know. I've got feelings, George, just as you have. But we've got a job to do so just concentrate on those poor devils who couldn't defend themselves. Right, Soldier?'

George Lucas didn't answer but stared ahead. He'd already made up his mind not to fire to kill.

Bill Roscoe stirred.

'There's movement down there, boss. Someone's come out of the bunkhouse. Do you think Johnny's been sussed?'

'Hardly likely. Johnny moves like a breath of air. Maybe it's a change of guard duty.'

'He's been gone a long time. Should one of us take a look-see and sharpen him up?'

'No. Anyone prowling about might get a knife in the ribs before he sees who it is. You know his reflexes. He's lethal.'

Joshua and young Skinner moved uneasily. The big black spoke under his breath, his deep voice still loud.

'I don't like it, boss. It's too quiet.'

'Then perhaps we should make for that clump of trees beside the corral and stay in shadow as much as possible.' Sabre glanced at the girl. 'You stay behind and keep out of this. It's none of your business.'

'But. . . .'

'I said, stay behind. That's an order!'

They rode quietly away, riding one behind the other and Carla watched them mingle with the shadows of outcrops of rock and the sparse scrub of the valley floor.

Then when all was quiet she grew uneasy and, cocking her rifle, she made up her mind to ride a little closer and watch and wait and, if all went well, she could always return to the original shelter.

Down in the valley, the men tethered their mounts well away from the building. Then after Sabre's instructions they fanned out, on the lookout for Johnny, creeping forward inch by inch, taking their time and waiting.

Suddenly the stout wooden door of the ranch-house was flung open and, as light streamed out, the watchers saw a body flung out crashing to the ground with a sickening thud. Instantly, a dark figure sprang through the door, gun aimed at the supine body. Then came a roar from inside.

'Damn you! Don't shoot him! I want to know everything he knows! I want to squeeze him dry!' A limping, bowed figure paused in the doorway and leaned clumsily against the jamb. 'I want to know why he was snooping and who for. We don't get many strangers in these parts!'

The gunman leaned over and pulled the Apache ex-scout to his feet and dunked him in the nearby horse trough. Sabre, watching, breathed a sigh of relief. For a ghastly few minutes he thought Johnny was dead. Johnny started flailing his arms, but a quick rabbit punch on the back of his head temporarily put him out.

Sabre gambled on a quick shot at the man in the doorway and missed. For a cripple, the ranch boss moved fast. The light went out and there was the sound of broken glass as window panes on both sides of the door were broken and then came the fusillade of shots.

The men inside fired indiscriminately and Sabre grinned. These were men who'd been living soft for a long while. This Wilbur J. Hawkes or Josiah B. Langford as he was now known, hadn't kept up the hard discipline necessary.

Ned Skinner's first bullet took out the burly man who'd knocked out Johnny. He was flung half in and out of the horse trough. Ned scrambled forward on his belly and managed to drag Johnny away out of sight.

Johnny groaned and shook his head.

'What the hell. . . .' He sat up, his head moving from side to side.

'Can't stop now, Johnny. You let yourself get caught.'

'Ah, yes, someone came out of the privy and the bastard hit me before I knew he was there.'

'It had to happen sometime, Johnny. You'll have to keep your eyes open in your ass after this!'

Then he was leaping away and Johnny took some deep breaths and crawled away to find

Sabre. He had some information to give him.

Sabre was deploying his men. Joshua was at the front holding back anyone who might make a run for it. Lucas was already circling the ranch house, and old Bill was holding back a bunch of cowboys trapped in the bunkhouse.

Sabre glanced at Johnny between shots.

'You all right, Johnny'

Johnny ignored the question. 'There's an old man, a woman and a girl inside as well as a couple of men. That feller's crazy. He's crippled, but he hasn't forgotten how to torture! Those women inside have been beaten, boss. He hotted up a goddamn poker and threatened to put my eyes out if I didn't talk. He seared my chest.' Sabre saw the long, angry, red burn through the torn shirt.

'The bastard! And Lucas was worrying about his conscience!'

'And there's another thing, boss.'

'Yes? What's that?' he said as he took another potshot at the window where a rifle barrel poked out. A yell followed. 'Another one down. I hope it was Hawkes.'

'There's a door at the far side near the corral. The bastard might try to get away.'

'Hell! Why didn't you say sooner.' Sabre made a run to the far side.

But he was too late. George Lucas arriving at the other side was in time to see a figure dive for one of the horses in the corral. By the lumbering gait he reckoned it was the man they were hunting.

'Stop or I'll shoot!' Lucas cursed himself for his hesitation as a shot came in return. He felt the powder burn as his hat flew from his head and then he saw the horse and rider take the corral poles at a flying leap and the horse was galloping as if goaded with spurs.

Lucas swore. Wilde would never forgive him if he ever knew he'd had the chance and hesitated. He was also angry with himself for nurturing the weakness in him. He was so sick of violence and living dangerously, all he craved for was peace. Would this war never cease?

Carla up on the rise and hidden in shadow heard the shooting and saw the gun flashes. She was frightened but curiously exhilarated.

She knew all about Wilbur J. Hawkes and the monster he was. She hoped he would get his comeuppance and none of the gang get hurt. She was already thinking of them as family, for during the time she'd been with them, they'd left her alone and treated her as one of themselves.

Then she saw the great horse leap the corral fence and Sabre standing out in the open and firing wildly and missing every shot.

Her heart pounded. It was now up to her. She had the advantage for the man riding so crazily would never expect trouble from up the valley.

She waited. Suddenly she was ice-cold. She had to get it right or the bastard would get away and

Sabre Wilde's surprise attack would come to nothing. She owed him. She must show her usefulness.

The horse pounded up the slope, the hunched figure spurring and using his reins to lash the horse's rump. Its head came up as if in pain as it slowed up the incline. Carla watched its progress and calculated exactly where man and horse should be when she broke cover.

Then, sick in her stomach but determined, she kneed her horse and they were both facing the oncoming man. She didn't think, she just acted. The rifle came up automatically and she had the hazy idea that she was aiming at one of the rats in her father's farmyard. She pulled the trigger and saw in savage triumph the twisted figure throw up his hands and catapult off the back of the now winded horse.

She started to tremble, a weakness overcoming her. She wanted to be sick but couldn't, and she was lying along her horse's neck when Sabre and his men came charging up the valley to her.

Sabre's eyes were shining when he reached her. 'You did it, girl! If it hadn't been for you he would have got away!' And those words were the last she heard for she flopped and slithered off her horse into Sabre's arms.

She never heard him say to George Lucas, 'By God! We've got as good a recruit as any man!'

She awakened, coughing and choking from a great slug of Johnny's rotgut whiskey. She was ashamed of her feminine weakness.

'I'm sorry, boss. I've never fainted in my life. I'll never do it again!' Her large brown eyes welled with tears.

Sabre patted her shoulder.

'You've never killed a man in cold blood either,' he said gruffly. 'I'm sorry it had to be you, but you did good, girl. We're all proud of you. From now on, you're one of us if you want it that way. Do you?'

She nodded, too emotional to speak.

FIVE

Carla crouched low over the fire, hands extended to the flames. She was exhausted but the Devil himself would never make her admit it. She would keep up with the men, despite blistered ass and knees, until she dropped from her horse, dead.

She wouldn't give Sabre Wilde the excuse to dump her.

She watched Joshua pour coffee into mugs. They'd eaten some two hours previously but hot coffee was a panacea at any time.

'Where's Sabre and Johnny?' she asked curiously.

'Taking a look-see,' old Bill answered laconically.

Carla saw Joshua give him a sharp glance. She also saw Lucas prowling the perimeter of the camp while young Ned snored with his hat over his eyes.

'Where are we? Why the caution?'

Bill shrugged. 'We're camped on the other side
of the hill to the railroad and there's lots of
comings and goings along the tracks.'

Joshua laid down the coffee-pot.

'Don't you trust the gal? Surely you can tell
her?'

'Tell me what?'

Bill looked at Joshua sourly. 'Orders is orders,
Joshua, but you wouldn't understand that, not
being in the army like.'

Carla drew a harsh breath. Now she knew why
this group was different. They were outlaws with
a difference. She'd heard whispers of the infamous
Colonel Quantrill who'd rampaged in Missouri in
the name of the Confederacy. Maybe Sabre Wilde
was another Quantrill but a deserter of the Union
Army? It was very puzzling.

'What's so important about the railroad?'

Old Bill sighed. 'Will you leave it, girl? If the
boss wants you to know, he'll tell you himself.'

'Tell her what, Roscoe?' Bill looked up to see
Lucas standing over him.

'She's wanting to know where the boss has
gone. It's none of her business.'

'She's one of us now, Roscoe. There's no reason
why she shouldn't know,' and he gave her a smile.
Bill looked on sourly, thinking Lucas would say
that. Everyone knew he was panting after her.
She could twist him round her dirty little finger if
she only knew it.

'I still say the boss himself should tell her,' he

answered sullenly. Lucas sighed irritatedly.

'Come, come. Why be so rigid? The fact is, Carla, he's gone to tap the telegraph wires and send a message to Washington. Johnny is watching his back. Satisfied?'

Wide-eyed, Carla looked at him. There were questions on the tip of her tongue, but something in Lucas's manner stopped her. What business could Sabre Wilde have in Washington?

Later, wrapped up in her blanket, she brooded, her feet pointing to the camp-fire when she heard horses' footsteps coming closer. She raised herself on an elbow and listened.

There was a mutter of voices as Sabre squatted and talked to Lucas and the old man. Though she strained to hear, they kept their voices low. She could only wait and watch.

She awakened, stiff and bruised, by a rough hand.

'Rise and shine, girl. We've got a whole heap of riding to do today.' She stared up into the face of young Ned Skinner who looked disgustingly fresh after a good sleep. She groaned. 'What is it, Carla? Can't stand the pace?' He grinned mockingly, for Carla had laughed at his advances, saying she wanted a man when she decided she needed one and not a boy. She struggled upright.

'Mind your own business, Ned,' she answered sharply. 'I can ride neck and neck with you, anytime!'

He laughed as he walked to the early-morning

fire and scraped strips of smoke-blackened sow-belly on to a tin plate and grabbed a hunk of pan bread. His laughter stiffened her determination and when she went to relieve herself behind a bush she examined her rear and the inside of the knees. The blisters had burst and she was appalled by the pus mixed with blood that was oozing from them. She firmed her lips. She'd rather die than betray her pain.

But Bill Roscoe guessed as she hobbled to the fire. 'You got blisters, girl?'

She nodded as she offered her plate for food.

Roscoe grinned. 'Don't worry. Keep 'em clean and they'll turn into corns. I suffered terrible when I joined the army. It was hell. After we've eaten I'll swab 'em for you with whiskey. That'll kill the bugs.'

'Won't it hurt?'

'Aye, stings like hell, but you'll get over it.'

He was right. Carla stuffed her fist into her mouth to stop the scream as he poured good whiskey over the sores. Then he gave her horse liniment and some rags and she patched herself up. When she went to saddle up, he followed her.

'You all right, girl? Not going to faint or cry or scream or act like one of those Washington females?'

'I don't know what kind they are, but I'm not one of them,' she answered grimly, but when she bestrode her mount she set her teeth as her weight hit the saddle.

He nodded.

'You'll do, girl. I've known grown men cry with saddle sores. Just remember, always keep your legs and rear clean and beware of stale sweat. Remember what the boss said: He'll not let you hold us up.'

'Where we heading for now, Bill?'

'To his own stamping ground, somewhere near Richmond in Virginia.'

'Why are we going there?'

'The boss has business there. Bad business.' Bill looked as grave as she'd ever seen him.

'Is it going to be dangerous?'

'Not any more than usual.'

'What you're trying to say is that he's got orders to execute someone?'

Bill started. 'How you know that, girl? And watch your mouth.'

'It wasn't hard to figure. He's doing for the Union what Quantrill did for the Rebs.'

'Don't class Sabre Wilde with that bastard! We don't loot lonely homesteads or rape women,' he said between clenched teeth. 'Talk like that and I'll paddle your ass, no matter how many blisters you've got!' He dug his heels into his horse's ribs and trotted to where Sabre Wilde was watching the last of the packhorses being loaded up.

'All set, boss, and we're ready to ride.' He gave a quick glance at the boss's grim face. Trouble for someone was brewing.

'Right, Roscoe. What's the girl's condition? I saw

you sloshing good whiskey over her.

He grinned. 'Yessir! Got new recruit's complaint, sir! Two days and she'll be toughened up.'

'No danger of her slowing us down?'

'None, sir. I must say she's a spunky kid. Got more spirit than some of those ranchers' sons we licked into shape.'

'Good! If she wants to ride with us, she'll need that spirit.' Then he leant down as Roscoe came nearer. 'Watch her, Roscoe. I don't fancy stripping her off and doctoring her up if she collapses.'

'Yes sir. I understand. I'll be like a mother to her!' and he saluted.

'Not so much of the saluting. Remember who we're supposed to be.'

Five days later, Carla was much easier in her rear and they unloaded the horses from the railroad train a day's ride from Richmond, Virginia.

Sabre Wilde took a deep breath. He was now on his home ground. It had been years since he'd left home. Mother and father dead and an only brother years older than himself who was determined not to share his inheritance. Horatio Wilde had been given a bag of gold eagles and told to go out there and make his own fortune. He'd joined the Union Army and made it up to major and after the war had been all set to make his mark in Washington.

That was until the day the new president earmarked him to handpick a handful of his best men to go underground and seek out and destroy the enemies of the United States, whoever they may be.

There was only one outcome for those men on the president's list. They had been tried and sentenced in their absence.

Death by execution.

Sabre Wilde, former major, was now living the life of an outlaw and his men with him.

But the latest name on the president's list was shattering him. It threatened to divide his loyalties. Surely there had been some mistake?

Once again, there conjured up the wisp of thought that had occurred to him at the very beginning of the assignment. Was the president paying off old scores and using him and his men as his personal bloodhounds?

He'd spent a sleepless night after he'd returned from intercepting the telegraph message over the telegraph wires. The staccato dots and dashes had been no mistake. He'd taken down the orders himself. He was an expert telegrapher.

How in hell had quiet, unassuming, Roger Cavendish got mixed up with those shadowy figures in Washington? And what had he done to deserve being hunted down and shot without warning?

It was seventeen years since he'd last seen Roger Cavendish who'd lived on a neighbouring ranch to Fallowfalls, the Wilde home. He'd been a good neighbour and Roger's son had been a year older than himself. The two families had spent much time together and had shared Christmas and Thanksgiving.

Sabre wondered about Nicky and what happened to him. He'd joined the Union Army and been wounded. Whether he was still alive, Sabre couldn't recall. Was this business something to do with Nicky?

As they lined up the horses beside the track and loaded up the pack animals, he found himself thinking of those carefree years as a boy when rounding-up cattle and breaking-in his father's horses was the only problem he had. He thought of his mother for the first time in years and remembered her clearly as a strong, no-nonsense kind of person, undemonstrative but exuding kindness and trust. He remembered the advice she often repeated.

'Horry, never take anything at face value. Always use your head, boy, and figure things for yourself!'

Now it was time to do just that. 'Thanks, Ma,' he muttered under his breath, 'I'll do just that.'

As they rode away from the railroad stop, he saw the land had not changed. In a curious way it was like stepping back in time. The advantage was he could now lead his little band across country, shunning the small communities, moving slowly on to his brother's land. There was a remote line cabin he was aiming for. An old tumbledown shack that the round-up hands used only during bad weather. The men had preferred sleeping out in the open under the stars. He remembered such nights with a rush of nostalgia which would have surprised Lucas and Roscoe if they'd known.

Sabre Wilde's heart was rarely worn on his sleeve. But he had a heart even if it was carefully concealed from the men who knew him.

The line cabin proved desolate with no sign it had been used in a long time. Lucas surveyed it with disgust.

'You mean we've got to hole up here?'

'Why not? Couldn't be safer. There's water running through those trees. We've got all we need. If you want to bed down outside you can do so. It's perfect.'

Lucas still showed his disgust. 'Well, if you say so, boss. You sure lead us into some muck holes. Have you thought of the location? Anyone coming into this bowl could have us fastened in.' He raised a hand and pointed out the rugged hills well studded with pine trees that surrounded this grassy valley.

'Yeh, well, I'm counting on no visitors, Lucas. In my time we only used the place twice a year at the most. Aw, quit moaning, Lucas. Nobody knows we're here. Just get your gear unpacked and we'll plan what we're going to do and I'll explain what the president's orders are.' Now he sounded grim and Lucas decided the protesting was over. This project had the boss worried and if he was worried there was something badly wrong.

The men set to with a will. Joshua found the old rock-built chimney still intact and no debris hindering the flow of air. He could cook there and foraged around looking for wood to burn.

Sabre gave orders for Johnny Eagle Eye to reconnoitre the surrounding country and report on any smoke signals or movement. Young Ned did his usual job of caring for the animals.

That left Lucas and Roscoe to squat under a tree and listen to Sabre's orders.

'Well, gentlemen, we've got another hit. . . .' He stopped as a shadow fell over them. Looking up, he saw Carla standing there, silent and waiting. 'Well?'

'What am I supposed to do? You've given me no orders.'

'Goddamn it! Couldn't you help Joshua or something? Women usually know what to do in camp!' Sabre spoke sharply. It still went against the grain that they had a woman with them. She bit her lip.

'I offered but he didn't want me around. Said I got in the way.'

'Did he, by God!'

Sabre made to rise but Lucas said quietly, 'Don't blame Joshua. Where he comes from white women don't do menial tasks.'

Sabre dropped down again and made up his mind.

'Sit with us, Carla. As you chose to ride with us and indeed you showed your courage, you may as well listen to what I have to say. But no comments mind! Understand?' She nodded and sat down cross-legged beside them, wincing slightly. Roscoe grinned.

'Ass still tender?' She nodded again, but kept her lips tight. Sabre cast her a humorous look, but ignored the exchange.

'Now that's settled, we can get on.' He looked round at them all. 'First of all, I want to say that I'm not happy about this. The orders are to go in and seek out Roger Cavendish and execute him forthwith. The charges are treason against the United States of America; receiving payment for information, helping Russian agents to infiltrate Washington society and causing unrest in Alaska with the object of blowing the Peace Treaty and the annulment of the purchase of Alaska from Russia. Evidently there are many people living up there who think Russia has betrayed them by turning the land over to America.'

'But the purchase has taken place!'

'Yes, but a lot of harm was done prior to the actual purchase. There were those in Washington who thought the purchase price could have been spent in better ways. Roger Cavendish has been accused and tried and sentenced in his absence.' Sabre looked around gravely. 'I knew Roger Cavendish when I was a boy. I can't see him as an agitator or a betrayer of his country.'

'So what do you propose to do?' Lucas eyed him steadily. 'I take it you're not prepared to ride into the homestead and use him for target practice?'

'Nope! This is one time I'm going it alone. I've figured it out. I want you, Lucas and Johnny to come as back-up. To keep watch but not interfere and I'm going in there to talk to Roger and get his side of this mess.'

'Is that wise? He could have changed a lot since you knew him, Sabre. He could be as guilty as the president says. After all, General Fothergill must have all the evidence.'

'I want to know the truth. Somehow all this smells. He has a son, Nicholas . . . his mother was Russian. . . .' Then he stopped and looked startled. Was that the connection? 'He and I were buddies from the age when we could fork our horses and visit each other's homes.'

'You mean you wonder if Roger Cavendish is covering up for his son?' asked Lucas shrewdly.

Bill Roscoe sat quietly, listening, not saying a word. Carla listened avidly, her eyes going from one to another.

'He could be. I hope not. I hope it's all a mistake.'

'Come off it, Sabre. You know damn well the president couldn't . . . wouldn't put a man on the list unless checked and double-checked!'

Sabre sighed. 'That's why I'm going in alone.'

'And if he's misguided enough to confess it's true, what then?'

'I'll shoot him. What else?'

SIX

The old man in the telegraph office glanced from one man to another and then back again at the big man with the silver star pinned on his chest. He was having a hard time holding on to his bowels.

'I didn't mean no harm, mister.' He licked his lips. These men, despite the presence of a star, looked tough and mean. No different really to the owlhoot gang who'd held him up two years come Michaelmas. These men had the same vicious look and wanted answers. 'Look, I thought it was one of the usual messages coming through. I swear it, mister. When I heard the receiver chattering, I thought it was the usual message coming through.'

'What made you know it was different?' Big Mal Buchan's eyes narrowed as the man hesitated. 'I want no lies. I can have you thrown in jail for collusion and helping an enemy of the state. You hear me?' The little man's head nearly wobbled off.

'Yessir! I hear you.' His voice was a croak. 'It didn't come through clear and there was answering flashes. I knew someone else was receiving and guessed it was someone hooking into the lines with one of them fancy thingamyjigs the engineers use.'

'And what exactly did you hear? When your boss reported what you'd heard, he sent me word. Now, tell me carefully what was said and where you think the person was who received the message.'

'I recorded the words termination and operation hunt and kill.'

'And where was this? Can you guess?'

The telegrapher's Adam's apple shot up and down and beads of sweat ran from his forehead.

'I don't know. I swear I don't on my mother's grave, God rest her! I don't know any more, just this hunt and kill stuff. I swear it.'

'Did you get a name, or are you making all this up? By God, if you're wasting my time I'll string you up!'

'No . . . no! It's all true! I think I heard the name Roger Cavendish but only once. I might have misheard.' He started to sob.

Big Mal looked at him with contempt. The poor little shit! He reckoned he was too frightened to lie. He made up his mind fast.

'Right, boys, we'll be on our way. We'll call on the local sheriff and see if he recalls a Roger Cavendish.' With that he swept out of the box-like office that stood beside the railroad track and his men followed.

Old Stinker Meadows lived up to his name when he finally realized that he was alone. He was getting too old. He couldn't stand the strain of strangers barging in. He felt as if he was going to have a heart attack and his bowels loosened. . . .

It was several days later when Big Mal finally rode into the Cavendish place. He cursed mightily when he heard of the shootout from the foreman and saw for himself the two fresh-dug graves some way from the ranch.

He resigned himself to a further search. He'd catch up with the bastard, Sabre Wilde and his gang before he was through. But the incident and the little he had gleaned from the old man had started a new train of thought. They'd not robbed Cavendish. The foreman had stressed that. It had seemed to the foreman like a deliberate execution. He was curious. Why had a good officer turned bad and taken his best men with him? Some day he would know.

Three hundred miles away, Sabre Wilde and his band were making their painful way back to their own particular haven. Lucas had a flesh wound in the shoulder and Roscoe a nasty cut from a knife. Carla was bruised. Her horse had stumbled and she'd been thrown. Sabre himself was unhurt. Now, as they travelled along, he went over the whole sorry affair again. It had been a clumsy victory, badly arranged and there was no satisfaction of a job well done. He was sick to his stomach. Never again should he be asked to involve himself with anyone he'd known in another life.

After a period of recuperation, he knew he must ask for an interview with General Fothergill. He was going to lay down some ground rules of his own. He deserved consideration and so did the men.

He and Lucas and Johnny had ridden off alone. His orders had been for the others to stay behind. He must confront Cavendish and the two men would keep watch and ride the perimeter of the ranch buildings. If they heard three shots in quick succession they should move in close and act according to the given situation, but not blunder into a trap.

At first, all had gone well. Sabre remembered the silence, the closed curtains and the dim light from a lamp. It was late and the moon was up and all was quiet in the bunkhouse, but Roger Cavendish was sitting up well beyond retiring time.

He'd eased his way in through the stout wooden door that had not been barred, Colt held high. He wanted to surprise Cavendish. He did, and he got a surprise himself, for there was a stranger sitting with Cavendish who was in the act of drinking whiskey and laughing at some joke. Both men started and the stranger tossed his glass aside and scrabbled for his gun.

Both men froze as Sabre had said icily, 'One wrong move and you're dead!' To prove it, he'd cocked the Colt that was trained on the stranger's stomach. 'You remember me, Cavendish?' As he had stepped into the light from the lamp, he heard Cavendish draw a sharp breath.

'Why, it's . . . it's Horatio Wilde, isn't it? It's been years since I saw you, boy. How are you? You sure gave me a turn.' He had half risen to his feet. 'It's all right, Ivan. He's a friend from way back. . . .'

'Hold your horses, Cavendish. Sit down and both of you keep your hands where I can see them. I'm not here as a friend.'

'Then what . . . ?' Cavendish had licked suddenly dry lips. 'Surely you're not here to rob an old friend of the family? I was your father's neighbour, for God's sake!'

Sabre had leaned against the edge of the long pine table facing the wide fireplace where logs burned merrily. Cavendish and the stranger were sitting in stiff-backed leather armchairs, one on each side of the hearth. The room was much more opulent than Sabre remembered it. Cavendish had prospered since those far-off days.

'Nope! I'm not into robbing my friends. I want some answers to some important questions,' he had said softly. 'For a start, introduce me to your friend.'

Cavendish had hesitated, his eyes flicking from his friend and back to Sabre.

'Oh, he's just passing through, Horry, my boy. Just an acquaintance, not a friend.'

'I'm here on delicate business, Cavendish. When a third party is present, I like to know all about them.'

'If it's like that, mister, I'll just get on my way and thank you kindly for your hospitality. I might see you again when I come into these parts.' With an easy smile, the stranger eased himself out of his chair. 'I'll get my horse and ride. Good luck to the both of you.' He'd given a mocking salute, picked up his hat and shoved it firmly on his head and swaggered out.

Sabre had let him go knowing his two watchdogs were out there waiting for any trouble to arise.

'Well? What is it, Horry? What do you want to know?'

'Is it true you're working as an infiltrator for the Russians?'

Cavendish, startled, had turned brick red.

'What the hell are you talking about?' he had blustered.

'Nicky, what is he doing these days and where is he?'

'What has Nicky to do with all this?'

'You tell me. I can't believe you would spy for the Russians without good reason. Is Nicky in trouble?'

'God damn it! You mind your own business, Horry Wilde! You can't come into my home and

accuse me of betraying my country without proof!
I'll complain to the governor! I'll ... I'll go to
Washington and complain to the president
himself! I'll have you hounded down. . . .'

'You can do that, Cavendish, but it won't do you
any good.' He withdrew a sheaf of papers from an
inner pocket and threw them down on the table.
'Look at them and tell me if they're all lies.'

Slowly, Cavendish had picked up some of the
top papers and read the contents. His face was
ashen as he read the accusations.

'My God, I never thought it would come to this!'
He had turned agonized eyes on Sabre. 'They've
got Nicky. His Uncle Vladovich came with a
message from his grandfather up in the Yukon.
He wanted to see Nicky and he hadn't much time
left. It was all a lie. It was the Alaskan Resistance
Group who wanted my help in Washington. They
knew I had influence to change the current policy.
There are many Russians living in Alaska who
are now designated as Americans and they refuse
their new status. There is much unrest.'

'Why don't they just go back to Russia?'

'Because Alaska is their home. Some of their
families have lived there for generations. Their
very livelihood is threatened. They are fishermen
and fur-traders but there has been a general
boycott of rebels' produce. Many of them are
starving.'

'And you go along with that?'

'For Nicky's sake. They have threatened to kill

him. I have only obeyed orders. . . !' He had
stopped abruptly as if he'd said too much.

'That man. You called him Ivan. Would his
other name be Zaracov by any chance?'

Cavendish started. 'How did you know?'

'A little bird told me.'

'What are you going to do now, Horry? I've told
you the truth. I'm a traitor I suppose, but not
because I want to be but because of Nicky. I'd do it
all again.' He had raised his head proudly and
thrown down the damning papers on to the table.

'I'm sorry, Cavendish. . . .'

It was then he recalled that all hell had broken
loose. Zaracov burst in through the door, two guns
outstretched just as Sabre was lining up his gun
on Cavendish's heart. Both guns spat fire seconds
apart. Sabre missed his target for he'd dropped to
the floor and rolled all at the same time. Zaracov's
bullets had embedded themselves in the pine-log
walls.

Cavendish, slow and dazed by events was now
searching for his weapon. Zaracov had pumped
slugs wildly as Sabre scrambled under the table
and the lamp exploded into fragments, oil drip-
ping everywhere. For a split second there was
sheer blackness and then with a gut-chilling roar
the air erupted into a sheet of flame.

Sabre had leapt for the window, Colt pounding
the glass and dived head first through it, jagged
shards of glass ripping his jacket and trousers.
The searing heat followed him. He heard screams

and somehow he had staggered away in the orange light cast by the fast burning ranch house.

Dimly he'd been conscious of rough hands hauling him away.

Then had come the worst horror of all. Out of the nearby bunkhouse spewed the cow hands, guns at the ready and, to Sabre's amazement, there had been a fusillade of shots coming from all around him.

He saw Zaracov stagger out of the door, lit up by the flames behind him. He heard Carla screaming abuse as her bullets went wild. But he was too engrossed in trading shots with the bewildered cowpokes. He saw two go down to his own guns and several more from his men around him.

They shouldn't have been there, he'd raged to himself. They'd disobeyed orders, but how glad he was they had done so.

He saw Johnny Eagle Eye's knife slice through the air and take a man in the throat, and Joshua holding a man above his head in the act of swinging him round to throw him at a giant of a man who had his sights on Lucas.

It was all split-second images, forgotten but recalled later as they rode away to lick their wounds and recover.

He had turned to watch Carla riding well behind, shoulders slumped, head down. He waited until she had drawn level.

'Carla, are you all right?' She had lifted a heavy head. She was dull-eyed.

'I didn't get him. I had him there in my sights and I missed the lucky bastard!'

'It was the glare of the fire, not you. It gave the wrong perspective. You'll get another chance.'

'Do you think so?' She hadn't sounded hopeful.

'I'm sure of it,' he had lied. He didn't tell her that the United States Marshal's Office and all Pinkerton agents were on the lookout for him. The chances were he'd be dead before she could spit.

'Next time I see him I'll be ready,' she had vowed. 'I have a feeling. . . .'

'Of what?'

She smiled wearily at him.

'That all this was meant to be. Do you believe in fate?'

'Nope! We have choices. We make our own destiny. By the way, whose idea was it to disobey my orders?'

She had smiled slyly. 'It was a joint decision. You can't blame Roscoe, Ned or Joshua. We all thought you were mad to want to go it alone with just Lucas and Johnny standing guard. You can be foolhardy, Sabre Wilde. You need looking after,' and with that sally, she had urged her mount ahead.

She had spoilt it though by looking back and saying pointedly, 'You didn't achieve your objective, Major. Couldn't you shoot him after all? He did die in the fire, you know!'

Sabre Wilde's jaw had clenched. So, someone had been talking. She knew he'd been a major in the army, therefore, maybe she knew about the president's involvement. He wondered who'd had the big mouth, Lucas, Roscoe or Skinner? Of the three, his guess would be Lucas who was sweet on her. Roscoe was too loyal to himself and Skinner hadn't been made privy to all the details of the assignment.

It meant that Carla must now stay with them. He couldn't afford to let her go.

He had tucked away the idea at the back of his mind that Lucas would be the most dangerous if too much pressure was put upon him. Maybe it would be better to ignore the captain's rank and put more trust in the old campaigner. Roscoe wasn't a fool and he was experienced and cool-headed in a crisis. Yes, in his own mind, Roscoe would be his number-one man.

Three more days' riding brought them to one of their regular hideouts. Carla was still moody and seething with hatred for Zaracov and the fact she'd missed her chance. She couldn't forgive herself. Her bruises, however, were healed and her blisters had dried up to scabs and she was riding easier.

Lucas and Roscoe both sighed with relief as for them it had been a nightmare ride. Johnny had gone ahead and scouted the area to be on the safe side. Nothing stirred. There was no giveaway smoke from a hidden camp-fire or the tell-tale signs of horses having been ridden in recently. The hideaway had not been used for months.

It was a cave in the side of a mountain, camou-flaged by a soddy structure that looked as if it was a tumbledown cabin used to stable horses. Horse droppings caked the floor and the whole place stank. Any stranger looking around would have turned up his nose and moved on.

But Sabre and his men had used this place before. It was ideal for their purpose, for, at the back of the shack, was the narrow opening of the cave. It meant each man had to stoop to get inside, but, once inside, the hole widened into a substantial cavern.

They'd had the forethought to stack the cave with a cache of staples for emergencies. This was only one of several hideouts they'd organized as they'd gone about the president's business.

Carla looked around in surprise when Roscoe found the tinderbox inside the soddy and lit a lamp that was half-hidden under stinking debris. She wrinkled her nose at the smell, but when the rock hiding the cave entrance had been rolled away and she stepped through into the cool, dank cavern, her spirits lifted a little.

Roscoe held the lamp high and the light seemed to disappear up into the vaulted shadows.

'What do you think of it?' he asked with a grin.

'I never would have believed it! It's fantastic!'

'It's better still when we gather pine boughs and make up real beds. The only thing we can't do is light a fire and water has to be carried from about a hundred yards away.'

'What about cooking?'

Joshua came over and laughed, his teeth showing very white in his black face.

'Quite easy, Miss Carla. This place has been an Indian stronghold and there's another opening further back. It leads to a rift in the rocks and someone built one of those beehive ovens that you seal up with mud. You fill it full of wood, get a good fire going and then you cook in the ashes when the rocks are hot. It makes wonderful sourdough bread and bakes jack-rabbits a treat!'

She looked about her as each man unloaded his gear.

'Where's Johnny?'

'Oh, he won't set foot in this place. He says it's haunted and the spirit of this place is unhappy that we are using it. He reckons we're defiling it.'

'How come?'

Roscoe swept round the lamp and highlighted one of the rough walls. There, in bright unfaded colours, were Indian paintings of hunting scenes and of sun worship and, in bolder colours than the rest, the hideous face of a mountain god with fire spewing from the top of his head.

'See, the mountain god himself, in all his glory!'

Carla looked at him in awe.

'He must have been a terrible god, erupting fire and smoke.'

'Yes, there are signs of ancient lava flows. Maybe the Indians had much cause to fear the wrath of the mighty god!'

'Come on, Roscoe, stop filling her head with myths. Let her choose where she wants to sleep and we can all get organized.' Lucas sounded weary. 'I could sleep for a month!'

They lay up for a week and recuperated. It took time to come down from the high generated by the tension created by the latest mission. It wasn't talked about. It was in the past, but each one of them was affected in some way or other. Lucas had bad dreams, and Sabre was filled with foreboding while Roscoe snapped at the others and lost his sense of humour. Only Joshua and Skinner were unaffected.

Johnny Eagle Eye spent his time alone in the woods and ranging the hills. He brought in the meat and ate with them outside the cave. Beyond that, he remained remote.

Carla herself spent her time near the stream, ready to run if strangers approached. No one came. She was as happy as she could be. She would be happier still if Zaracov was dead. . . .

Sabre Wilde looked and watched, noting the demoralization of his men. Now that Lucas and Roscoe's wounds were nearly healed, he knew it was time to move on and give them the relaxation they needed with women, and he knew the very place to head for. . . .

SEVEN

The old saddle-tramp shifted the wad of tobacco from one cheek to the other as he crouched over his fire, his eyes narrowing as he watched the little band of men picking their way through the scrub towards him.

He shifted warily, his right hand feeling for the old shotgun tucked away behind him. His old heart beat a little faster as he surveyed the riders who looked as if they'd ridden hard and fast.

They were a bearded, scruffy bunch, more wild than the small band he'd seen heading north two days ago. He'd watched their passing from a high altitude, hidden by rocks and the scrub that his mules enjoyed.

He was a loner, enjoying the freedom of the wild country. He didn't ask for much. He was too old to have goals and ambition. Now he felt the newcomers were a threat to his freedom.

He spat into his fire and heard the sizzle of the gob. Damn the pesky bastards! Why had they had to stumble over his tracks and seek him out?

The men drew nearer and old Tom took heart. He saw the gleam of a tin star on their leader. He relaxed. It was a posse after all, not a bunch of hoodlums, although they looked it.

'Howdy, stranger!' The leader gave what he thought was an ingratiating smile. 'Saw your trail and thought we'd stop off and visit for awhile.'

The smile was that of a wolf. Tom's eyes narrowed again. This bunch didn't smell right. He hawked and spat another gob of brown tobacco-stained juice into the fire.

'Howdy, yourself. I've got coffee brewing, but I'm plumb out of eats. I gotta catch me my next meal if I want to eat. You're welcome to warm yourselves and drink my coffee.'

With that, he waited, his hand feeling the comfort of the old shotgun.

The men dismounted and stretched. One of them fumbled for a bottle and took a swig before digging out a tin mug and pouring the thick stewed coffee that old Tom loved.

'And where might you be heading for, mister?' he probed, as the man with the tin star crouched down beside him. The man laughed.

'Any which way. We're on the prod. We're trailing a bunch of outlaws. Seen any activity around here?'

Old Tom's eyes flickered before he answered.

'Nope! Silent as the grave. Only me, Betsy and Joey and that's how I like it!'

The man leaned nearer.

'And what if I say you're lying, mister? We've been following tracks and lost them by the river. You must have seen or heard something!'

'Nary a thing, and I can swear on my old man's chances in hell! I don't go looking for trouble. All I'm interested in is something for the pot. I don't need company, mister.'

'But you've got eyes and ears. And there isn't a man living who isn't curious if he sees a bunch of riders passing by.'

Suddenly a mighty hand caught Tom by the scruff of the neck and forced his head between his legs. He felt the bones in his back stretch and protest. It was as if his spine would crack in two. He screamed in agony.

Then his head was being dragged up. His eyes were staring in their sockets as sweat poured down the stubbly grey beard.

Then again his head was forced down but this time he was dragged nearer to the fire.

'You'll tell me what I want to know or next time your face will kiss the flames!' Then he was flung on his back, sweating and heaving.

He watched the wolf smile above him, feeling dizzy. He was too old for this. He didn't know the identities of that bunch who'd ridden by, so why protect them from these men?

He knew the answer to that. One of them had been a woman and some long forgotten memory of another time, forbade him from betraying a woman to these men.

He knew they would never let him live, despite the tin star. These men were killers, first and foremost. He'd seen their like before.

'I don't know anything,' he groaned and, as strong hands forced him upright and down into the flames, his last thoughts were of Betsy and Joey, and what would happen to them. . . .

'Goddammit!' Mal Buchan looked down at the smoke-blackened face. 'I was sure the old fool must have seen something.'

'Maybe they rode through the night,' Mitch Two Rivers opined as he took another swig from his bottle.

'And you can put that away,' growled Big Mal. 'We'll all have to cast around and look for sign. So get to it, all of you.'

'How about some grub first? I bet the old feller was lying. He'll have some staples on the pack mule. I'll take a look.' One of the Macklyn boys approached a mule which lashed out angrily and caught Jock Macklyn with a sharp kick on his knee. He yelped and cursed as the other men laughed. Swiftly he drew his gun and, flushed with anger, shot the beast in the head. His agonized braying as he flung up his head and collapsed sent the other mule into a frenzy as it smelled the freshly spilled blood. Nostrils flaring, eyeballs rolling and ears flapping, Betsy's yellow teeth caught Macklyn on the shoulder. With a yelp, he was wrestled to the ground and before any of the watching men could intervene, Jock Macklyn's face was pulped by plunging forelegs.

'The sonofabitch!' bawled Jock's brother. 'Someone do something!' His voice released them from their momentary paralysis and their guns barked in quick succession.

But it was too late for Jock. He lay in a pool of blood, his face unrecognizable.

Stunned, the men watched Hamish Macklyn kneel beside his brother and sob. Then Big Mal spat in the dust and turned away.

'You boys'd better help Hamish to bury Jock good and deep. He deserves it!' he said as he stared out across the valley. 'Get to it, boys. Time's a-wasting and we've got to find those tracks!'

It was time to move on. The boys were becoming uneasy and jittery. Lucas bullied Skinner because he suspected Skinner of cosying up to Carla, and Roscoe and Joshua were at loggerheads over the running of the camp. Roscoe was irritable with everyone and Sabre found himself increasingly short-tempered.

Now that the men's wounds had healed, they were suffering from boredom. It was time to ride and make for Baldarosa and that notorious town's famous saloon, The Baldarosa Belle and the bunch of women who were famed all through the territories as lively companions intent on easing a man's frustrations at a price. They had visited before, mingling with adventurers, gamblers and lawbreakers and had brushed shoulders with other cut-throat gangs hiding out from the law.

It was a community that was always changing. It was a miserable town made up of timber shacks with one straggly street and a number of buildings erected wherever man's fancy had taken him. The Baldarosa Belle was the most ornate, run by the man who owned the only store in town. Hank Whittle virtually owned the town and the men who flocked to it. His freight wagons kept the town alive. He brought in women, food stocks, guns and ammunition and all could be bought at outrageous prices.

He prospered because those who came and sought him out needed his help. They grumbled behind his back and called him a rat-faced chiseller for exploiting them, but they knew he had the advantage.

Now he watched the little cavalcade ride down the street from his rocking chair on the veranda of The Baldarosa Belle. He drew on the Havana cigar that he clasped between his teeth and blew smoke into the air.

'Lovey,' he shouted, in a stentorian voice that suited his fat body, 'come and see who's riding in. There'll be trouble tonight, I'll be bound!' and he gave a great belly laugh that shook his whole frame.

Rosie Lovett eased herself through the batwings and watched the slow deliberate progress of the men who walked their horses abreast and oblivious to the townsfolk who had to get out of their way.

'By God! If it isn't Sabre Wilde!' Lovey's eyes narrowed. 'And who the hell is the woman with them?' Hank detected a note of jealousy in her voice. It amused him. Gone were the days when he'd kept Rosie Lovett for his exclusive use. Now he was more interested in money and power than one woman. He would rather down a bottle of his imported whiskey.

'We'll soon know then the rest of the town will. Goddammit, she's young and a good-looker! I wonder if she would consider staying on here permanently. We could do with some fresh faces!'

Lovey scowled. 'Don't you dare even consider it!' she snarled. 'We've just got rid of that last bitch who stirred up trouble with the girls. I don't want to run another out of town tarred and feathered!'

'Aw, Lovey, you were a bit mean about her. God knows what would have happened to her if that big bruiser with the eye-patch hadn't come along and offered to take her away with him.'

'Serve the bitch right! I hope the tar took the skin off her! It'll teach the girls not to take other women's men!'

'God knows what the fuss is about; there's plenty of men for all of you girls. It's a wonder any of you can sit down!'

'Now, Hank, you know you love it when we're busy. You get your percentage and we get protection.'

'Talking of percentages, you'd better go warn the girls that the Wilde gang are in town.' He heaved himself out of his chair and moved to the veranda steps as Sabre Wilde drew up and prepared to dismount along with his men.

'Howdy, Sabre Wilde. It's a long time since you passed this way. Come in; drinks are on the house, boys. You'll be wanting rooms and some grub.' He opened the batwings wide. Then he squinted at Carla, taking in the long, blue-black hair tied back with a piece of shirt-tail torn from the check shirt that was many sizes too big for her and the ill-fitting canvas pants that accentuated her femininity.

'Now who might this little waif be? Or shouldn't I ask?' He gave Sabre a lewd wink.

Sabre gave him a hard stare and put an arm about Carla's shoulder and drew her inside as the men behind them tethered the horses and Lucas, with a closed-in sullen look, saw to Carla's.

'She's not one of your class of women, Hank. Remember that. She's got claws, too, so don't let any of your customers get the impression she's easy. They could get a nasty surprise, eh, Carla?'

Carla looked up at him and laughed and quietly drew the gun half concealed under the shirt. Hank looked at it and licked his lips.

'Can she use it, or is it for show?'

'Too damn right she can use it! She's killed a man at sixty paces!'

'Hell! She must be some gal.' Hank backed off

and waddled over to the watching barman who was mopping up his bar-top.

'Give the boys what they want, Charlie. It's all on the house.'

Charlie nodded. 'What's it to be, fellers?'

Rosie Lovett descended the stairs, the rest of the girls following behind. They'd hastily tidied themselves up, drenched themselves in cheap perfume and were now on their way to greet the newcomers.

Sabre's voice had carried and Rosie felt affronted at the reference to that flat-chested slip of a girl being far superior to herself and the other girls. She raged inwardly although she smiled and sailed down the stairs with arms outstretched, her hennaed hair puffed and curled and showing little tell-tale streaks of grey at the roots. There were more lines on her face than Sabre remembered.

'Darling,' she screeched, 'you've come back to me! How long is it? Two years or is it three?'

She flung her arms about him and kissed him on the mouth. 'My dream man. There's never been a night when I haven't wondered when you would come back. And now you're here!' She leaned back and gazed up at him, her hand stroking the beard and following the cicatrix on his cheek.

He whipped his head back and looked down at her with some distaste. Under the perfume she smelled stale and she'd been eating garlic. He put her gently from him.

'Hello, Lovey, you're looking good.' She preened and pressed her well-corseted bosom into his chest.

'I take it you'll be coming to visit me when you've washed and eaten?' she grinned suggestively.

'Not tonight, Lovey. I've got business to attend to.'

She pouted and stroked his shoulder. 'What could be more important than sharing a bottle with me and maybe. . . .' Her voice tailed off suggestively.

'Like I said, sweetheart, I got business. Maybe you would entertain my boys?'

She swung away from him in a temper.

'It's her, isn't it? You've gone and saddled yourself with that . . . that skinny-chested whore!' She made a dive at Carla who stepped back, eyes glinting. She made a gesture to draw the heavy gun at her side.

'Careful, Carla!' said Sabre sharply, as he grabbed Rosie Lovett's flailing arm. He shook her like a ragdoll and as Rosie opened her mouth to scream, slapped her across the cheek hard enough to shock her into silence.

'What in hell's the matter with you, Lovey? Why the tantrum? I'm not one of your regular guys!'

Rosie turned her head away as he held her. Tears were in her eyes. How could she tell him she'd had a fantasy dream about him for two years? That he had been the most gentlemanly man she'd taken to bed and that she'd used him as a yardstick against other men? She'd hoped he would come back, and now he had, with a slim young trollop with him. No wonder she'd gone berserk with disappointment.

'I'm sorry,' she said humbly. 'It won't happen again. I don't know what got into me.'

'So you should be sorry. Apologize to the lady.' She looked up sharply, but his face was grim. She looked around at the gawking men and the other girls. Two of them were trying vainly to hide malicious smiles. Rosie wasn't the most popular girl around. Even the four cowboys sitting around a table playing cards had stopped to watch the ruckus. Only Whiskey Pete lay oblivious with head on arms and out for the count.

'Well?

She took a deep breath and faced Carla reluctantly.

'I'm sorry. It shouldn't have happened.'

Carla gave her a long cold stare and then nodded and turned her back.

'If you don't mind, Sabre, I'd like to find me a room and take a bath, if it's possible in this one-horse crap-heap of a town!'

Hank Whittle flushed. He was proud of his town. It had taken a lot of sweat, skulduggery and gun-toting to get it as it was today. He was the kingpin, the man who pulled wires and allowed those who sought asylum to stop or go; some of them had stayed planted for ever. They were a

warning that nobody messed with Hank Whittle.
They also helped to fill Boothill and give a certain
history to the place.

'Hey, miss, watch your mouth! This is one of the
safest hideaways in the whole of the territory.
We've got more wanted men here in Baldarosa
than any government slammer!' He spoke
proudly. 'No US marshal has ever tried to ride in
here and take his man, and not even the military
would get near enough to blow us to hell! Think
on it, miss: you're safe here.' He grinned, showing
yellow, crooked teeth.

She stared at him, lips curling.

'Huh!' She turned and went through the swing
doors and, once outside, she took several deep
breaths.

The men watched her go with differing reac-
tions.

Lucas swallowed his drink and with great
nonchalance walked after her. He knew exactly
how tinder-dry tempers were in this woman-
scarce town.

Roscoe watched her with admiration. A great
little filly was the girl, with a heart like a lion.
She was going to take some controlling. He would
have liked her for a daughter.

Ned Skinner watched her, laughed and ordered
another beer, his eye already on a dark little filly
peeping at them from the landing above.

Sabre gave her a glance, concluded Lucas would
find her a billet, and concentrated on Whittle.

'Take no notice of the female, Whittle,' he said casually. 'She's poison. She'd rampage after your girls, spoil their looks and spoil your trade. A regular little tartar, jealous as hell and only happy when she's causing trouble.'

'Is that so?' Whittle looked at the scarred man curiously. 'Did she do that?'

Sabre put a hand up to the jagged cicatrix showing through the beard. He nodded.

'Another one of those and one for yourself,' he said and hunched over his glass. 'Tell me,' he went on softly, 'any lone strangers come into town within the last few days?'

Hank Whittle looked at him shrewdly.

'Looking for someone special?'

'You might say that, but I'm interested, is all.'

'There was a feller rode in a couple of days ago. Wounded he was. His arm all crocked up and swelled like he had lead poisoning. He wanted a sawbones and had to settle for old Billy Two Feathers who rattled his bones over him, lanced his arm and charged him a couple of bottles of my best grog. He paid up and left town.'

'Was he a foreigner? A Russian, maybe?'

'Could have been. Talked funny like a trapper or some such.'

Sabre nodded. 'Thanks, Whittle. Probably the man I'm interested in. Did anyone see him leave?'

'Not as far as I know. Maybe he told Billy where he was heading.'

'And where does he hang out?'

'Along the street, next to the Chink who washes laundry for those who're particular-like and the old whore who lets rooms and cooks for anyone who'll pay.'

Sabre drank up and nodded to the boys who were watching the card game.

'I'll go and grab us some rooms. You can follow when you're ready. There's an old woman next to the Chink. We'll doss there.'

He drew deep breaths of fresh air when he left the stuffy saloon. He would go find this Billy Two Feathers who was good at healing. Apart from Carla's experience with Zaracov, he wanted the man himself. He had to know about his involvement with his friend, Nicky Cavendish. He'd tear the truth from Zaracov, even if he had to resort to Indian methods. . . .

The Baldarosa Belle gradually filled up. A scrawny old man with beautiful hands started playing on an old tinny piano and it was the signal for a rousting night in the saloon. The men tumbled in, sweaty and eager to see the Baldarosa women put on an impromptu show. They were the same songs and the same dance routines, but the men didn't mind. They liked to see the legs encased in long cotton bloomers with a hint of black stocking kicking high and giving tantalizing glimpses of thighs and, if you were lucky, other unmentionables. Most of the men settled for that. Few could pay the high prices to sleep with the women. They watched and salivated and lusted and lost themselves in a fog of alcohol to fantasize in their dreams.

The women enjoyed teasing the men, but now all of them vied for the newcomers. They were no longer friends, they were rivals.

Hank Whittle grinned with satisfaction. His barman and his girls were doing a roaring trade, thanks to the Wilde gang.

Lucas had joined them after seeing Carla settled in a clean but barely furnished room, which was luxurious compared to what they were used to.

He grinned when he saw old Roscoe fighting off the advances of a fat woman nearly as old as himself and dressed loudly in purple. Her pudgy fat hands were all over him causing his face and neck to redden. Lucas declared loudly that he'd never seen him so frightened, not even in battle.

Ned Skinner was loving the attention of two young girls. The girl he favoured was the pretty young thing who'd been peeping and smiling at him earlier. The other girl was blonde and her hair rippling down her back covering her bare shoulders fascinated him. He wished he could afford both.

They were Kitty and Amy and they looked and smelled like flowers. They liked their beer, too, and soon Ned's head was swinging. He felt on top of the world. Hot lips sent tingling shocks through his system.

'What about coming upstairs now?' Kitty whispered in his left ear.

'Take no notice of her, come with me,' Amy's husky voice breathed into his right ear. 'I'll teach you some tricks you'd never believe.'

Ned tried to focus his eyes on Amy's blue ones. God, she was every bushman's dream. A vision conjured up by a lonely camp-fire. He sighed. Surely he was dreaming. This couldn't be true. Two of 'em begging him . . . suddenly through his befogged gaze, the two girls were torn from him. Screaming, they hit the floor at the side and at the back of him. He shook his head. What the hell? And then a meaty fist landed squarely on his jaw and he saw stars as he was flung from the rickety chair and landed on the dirt floor half on top of Kitty, legs entwined in frothy petticoats which made it difficult to regain his feet. Another punch took him on the side of the head, but he saw it coming and rolled with the blow and was up in time to see the big stranger drag Amy from the floor and slap her face as he roared, 'I'll teach you to make up to every bit of scum that rides into town!'

The saloon had gone quiet except for a couple of girls who screamed and scrambled out of the way. The other drinkers waited with interest to see what would happen next. The scrawny young stranger didn't look like a fighting man. Big Barney made mincemeat of cocky young blades who crossed him.

Crouching, Big Barney turned back to Ned.

'As for you, mister, I'm gonna teach you a lesson. You can't come into this here town and take our women, willy-nilly!' He moved fast. He didn't give Ned time to shake his head.

'But they're whores. . . .' Ned's protest was drowned in a flurry of movement and sound as a jolt to his ear exploded inside his head. He staggered back and then red-hot rage engulfed him and he catapulted himself forward, his long gangly figure suddenly all hard muscle and gristle.

Big Barney wasn't expecting trouble. His height and girth were usually enough to intimidate any fool who tangled with him. He was heavy on his feet and he took Ned's first two punches as if Ned was pounding a rock wall.

Lucas had stepped forward impulsively to join the combat but Roscoe's warning hand stayed him.

'Give the boy a chance,' he growled. 'It's his fight. We can always wade in if the dirty tricks get too bad. He glanced round for the others. Joshua and Johnny Eagle Eye were drinking alone in a corner. Joshua caught Roscoe's eye and nodded. Roscoe knew they were both ready for action.

Big Barney tried to get Ned in a bear hug. He was nearly successful, but Ned caught him a vicious crack on the shin which made him howl. Then Ned came in with head down, punching hard against the big man's paunch which caused him to jack-knife, then Ned's fist connected with his chin.

The makeshift bar collapsed as the heavy body landed with a thump. Glasses and bottles went skittering causing broken glass to cascade in all directions and liquor to spill from broken bottles.

It was then Hank Whittle took a hand. He cold-cocked Ned from behind with a bottle and, as Ned went down, Lucas and Roscoe decided simultaneously that now was the time to act.

An Apache yell and a stentorian shout from the deep-chested Joshua froze the blood of all those who heard the combined battle cry. Then they, too, were in there, fighting their way to stand elbow to elbow with Roscoe and Lucas to give Ned time to recover.

In an instant, the earlier camaraderie of the saloon was gone. It was a signal for everyone to get into the fight. Those with grudges fought amongst themselves. Hank Whittle roared for them to stop but none heard him. Someone caught him in the mouth and he spat out a tooth. It was every man for himself. The girls were now standing on the stairs and several got in some good blows to the men below, using their stout buckled boots. It was a fight retold for many years to come.

EIGHT

Sabre Wilde lounged in the rickety wooden chair, his feet resting on the raised foot of a narrow, makeshift bed. He was watching with interest Carla bathing Ned Skinner's wounds, a grin playing across his mouth.

'Then what happened when this guy took a punch at you?'

'Came at me like a maddened steer, that he did. All hell broke loose and before you could spit, everyone had joined in.' Ned jumped as Carla pressed a little too heavily on a cut on his forehead. 'Hey! Watch it, girl. That hurt!'

'Serves you right for getting mixed up with those whores!' she answered tartly. 'Even I know newcomers should suss out which way the land lies when it comes to tarts. They've all got their protectors. . . .'

Ned screwed his face round to look at her. 'How d'you know that? Is there something we don't know about you?'

She glared at him and slapped his face. He ducked and yelled.

'Ow! I'm one of the walking wounded, remember?'

'Then mind your manners! If you want to know, I heard Pa and some of his drinking cronies talk when they thought I was out of the way. Most of those tarts have regular fellers and when their men are out of town, they make extra cash on the side. If you don't believe me, ask for yourself . . . if you dare!'

Sabre laughed. 'She's right, Ned. Always check out the watering-holes before moving in. There could be wild animals or men depending on the type of watering-hole. It pays to stand back and drink quietly and wait and watch.'

'But those gals were all over me! How was I to know?'

'Instinct, boy. You should have tumbled when none of the locals was sniffing down their necks! They were taking a chance. I understand Big Barney was out of town and not due back for some days. He came back early. Amy's not a pretty sight; she'll not be down in Hank's bar for several days.'

Ned sighed. 'You could have warned us, boss!'

'The others knew. I thought you did.'

'But you promised us women, boss.'

'Yes, but at the right time. You should have stuck to drinking and waited for Hank's all clear.' He grinned again. 'Let this be a lesson to you.'

'Ah, well, the others enjoyed the ruckus and so did the locals.'

'I doubt if we've heard the last of it. They say Big Barney is a bad man to cross and he's got a long memory.' He sounded grave.

'What's that mean, boss?'

'It means you have to have eyes in your ass, boy, and so have we all. Big Barney belongs to a very mean outfit which hangs out on the edge of Baldarosa and controls the trails coming in and out.'

'Hell! We might have trouble leaving?'

'Yeh, but I'm sending Joshua and Johnny out to scout around and if there's an Indian trail out, Johnny will find it.'

'You think it could be that bad, boss?'

'I don't think, I know. This town isn't one of your cow towns full of cowboys and prospectors. They're all on the run and will stop at nothing. If Big Barney gets the whole town behind him, we could be in for a tough deal.'

'Hell! I thought we was in for some fun and games.' Ned sounded disappointed. 'I thought it was gonna be drinking and women and some gambling on the side, like it was in Wichita.'

'Wichita's different. That's a regular cow town. Baldarosa was spawned by outlaws for outlaws and they don't play by the same rules. It's the power of the gun here, Ned, and don't forget it. Hank Whittle keeps that power in his own two hands.'

'Then why bring us here, boss?'

'Oh, you need the break. We all do, but there were other reasons. Rubbing shoulders and listening to the bar-room gossip could be useful.' Sabre's boots came down heavily to the floor. 'Now listen, kid, and listen good. We wait and we watch and we keep our noses clean. Lucas and Roscoe are out now listening for news of Big Barney. We think he's left town to meet Holy Joe Stavinsky whom he rides with.'

Ned breathed heavily and Carla paused in her bandaging.

'Holy Joe!' Ned sounded choked. 'I've heard of him. He's the one who recites the Bible before he shoots a feller. Got this thing about damnation and the fires of Hell!'

'Yeh, he does that all right, but one of these days he's going to face a man who gets in first while he's spouting his claptrap. But what is interesting, is his name, Stavinsky. Now what do you make of that?' Sabre gave Carla a sideways look. He reckoned she would cotton on faster than Ned. She did. She was a smart girl, was Carla. She laughed.

'You're a crafty devil, Sabre Wilde. You're after Zaracov, aren't you? Stavinsky's Russian and you figure he would go to ground with him?'

Sabre nodded. 'If he's still in these parts I could bet my best pair of boots that he's with Holy Joe.'

'And that's why you gave the boys the spiel about having a liquor and woman binge in Baldarosa?'

'Yeh, and Ned here's just about ruined the whole project.'

Ned looked hangdog. 'Sorry, boss. My brains were in my trousers!'

Sabre shrugged. 'My fault. I played it too close to my chest. I didn't think things would move so fast. Well, all might not be lost. We'll wait and see which way the cat jumps when Holy Joe rides into town. Meanwhile, enjoy a drink but keep your wits about you. I don't know just how thick Hank Whittle is with Holy Joe. There might be spies from both sides watching you. You'll be Big Barney's target and he's bound to have friends. Keep with the others, Ned, and watch your back!' He got up and stretched. Carla was curious.

'And what are you going to do, Sabre?'

'Mosey down the street, try a few bars and maybe call on Miss Rosie Lovett.' He grinned as Carla's eyes spat fire.

'Huh! That whore! What's she got that I haven't, eh?'

'It's not what you think, Carla. I want information and Rosie's the one to tell me. She's getting on and knows that she's not got much longer pulling in the punters. She'll sing all she knows for a fat roll of greenbacks!'

Carla pouted and rough-handled Ned who got out from under.

'And what am I supposed to do in this goddamn place?'

'I don't know. What do women do when they come into town? Go buy yourself something pretty from Whittle's store and listen to the women's gossip. Use your imagination!'

She threw her chin in the air as he laughed and walked out of the room. She turned to Ned furiously.

'And what are you grinning at?'

He shrugged, still laughing.

'I wouldn't set your sights on him, Carla, he's old enough to be your daddy. Besides . . . he likes 'em mature, when he likes 'em!'

'And how often's that?' She hated herself for asking.

'Not often. He's an iron man is our boss. He's choosy, but when he chooses, oh boy! Does he choose well!'

Carla hunched her shoulders. 'I don't give a damn about him! He's just a . . . a. . . .' She was lost for words to describe him.

'An ice-cold cuss? A hard-to-get macho man you'd like to snatch from Lovie?' He gave the name the pronunciation Hank Whittle had used, a long drawn-out Le. . .er. . .rv. . .ee. Carla flung the rest of the bandages at him.

'Dog's breath! Here, do the rest yourself! I don't know why I bother!'

'Because you love me!' he called after her, and he laughed again when she gave a rude sign.

'Asshole!'

*

Joshua waited with the two horses in the shadow of an overhanging boulder as Johnny Eagle Eye climbed the escarpment to look into the next valley for any movement. The surrounding country was a mixture of green valley with high-rising foothills of scrub ending in a series of canyons, ideal for hideouts, stolen cattle and lonely ranches where a man could hide forever.

They'd been gone two days and a night and travelled many miles, following narrow streams and old Indian trails, with Johnny always looking for sign of recent movement. There were signs aplenty, but not of recent passage. Twice they thought they'd found paydirt when they spied lonely tumbledown shacks, but the fires had been long dead and horses' hoofprints hard and crusted, droppings rock hard and desiccated.

Now Joshua waited hopefully. This was country they'd never crossed before. There had been signs of a bunch of steers being driven this way, but the signs had ceased abruptly at the edge of a fast-flowing river. It was a ford, but on the other side were no tracks.

They'd followed the river for several miles both ways and found themselves in a canyon which deepened as they went. The river was now a rushing torrent. Where the hell had those animals gone?

He heard Johnny shout and tethered the horses

and came out into the shaft of light streaming down from above.

'Hey, Joshua, get your ass up here!' The excitement in the usually inscrutable Johnny's voice made him scramble up quickly.

He arrived beside Johnny panting.

'This had better be good,' he said as sweat ran down his black face, making it look like polished ebony.

The Indian grimaced. It was meant to be a smile but just twisted his facial muscles. Joshua stared at the leathery, pitted features in astonishment. The strongly carved face with the big hooked nose looked nearly human.

'You all right?' Then Johnny really did surprise him. His lips stretched into a wide wolf's grin.

'We got paydirt, black man. Look over the rim and see for yourself.' He danced a little jig, but then became the remote Apache that Joshua recognized.

Joshua took off his wide-brimmed hat and cautiously took a quick peep. His eyes bulged and he, too, started to grin.

'By God, that's the biggest spread I've seen in years! That must be Holy Joe's watering-hole! No wonder that miserable clutch of shacks that calls itself a town survives out here! Hank Whittle must be the key man who brings in Holy Joe's supplies!'

They looked down on a verdantly green valley, watered by the same wide river they'd followed.

But now it gushed through a narrow opening which it had carved out for itself over thousands of years and now tumbled down through the valley feeding the good pastureland. The surrounding hills sheltered the area from winter storms.

The sprawling ranch house was surrounded by other buildings laid out in military fashion. There were corrals for horses, a mill by the river and signs of logging on the far slopes. Cattle grazed farther down the valley. Joshua spat.

'I bet those cows have mixed brands and they don't look as if they've walked very far. They're fat and ready to move out.'

Johnny Eagle Eye silently pointed to the right, way above them. Joshua caught the gleam of binoculars.

'Shit! They've got guards on the lookout!' and they both ducked down below the rim of rock.

'We go. We report to the boss.'

'We've seen no signs of Big Barney. Maybe we should try and get closer.'

'No, we go now.' Johnny pointed in another direction and this time they had been seen. A hum of an angry bee passed close to Joshua's head and then came the sharp, unmistakable sound of a repeating rifle.

Johnny didn't wait but scrambled down the escarpment, Joshua following. The horses pricked their ears and raised heads and whinnied as the two approached for a fast getaway.

They rode by the river which tumbled into the mountainside.

'So the underground river is the way into the valley. They drive the cows to the ford and hold 'em, then drive so many at a time up the riverbed itself and through the tunnel and into the valley and then the critters make their own way down into the pastures,' Joshua mused as they rode along.

'So that would be how the boss would go in?' The two men looked at each other and Joshua gave a laugh of triumph while the carved totem pole that was Johnny's face, took on its fierce grimace.

Sabre Wilde accepted another drink from Rosie Lovett. It hadn't been hard to persuade her to talk. A flash of a billfold, a hint of payment for information and Rosie had looked around the near empty saloon and behind her battered fan she whispered, 'Make like you've just propositioned me.' Immediately he leaned over her and whispered in her ear and, putting a hand on her bare shoulder, pulled her close and gave her an enthusiastic kiss on her mouth.

She looked at him shrewdly.

'I think you enjoyed that. What about coming upstairs, mister?' She nodded towards the wooden stairs.

He got up eagerly and followed, her over-ripe

bottom swaying seductively in the soiled green gown that had seen better days.

'Well . . . whadya know!' said one of the men huddled around a card table, 'our Lovie's got herself a man.'

'He must be hard-pressed for a woman,' said another.

'Or too frightened of Big Barney and his pals,' another grinned.

'He's a better man than me,' said another. 'She wants a pillowcase over her face.'

'Aw, don't be like that,' said another, who was known to go with Rosie when his itch couldn't wait.

'I bet you five dollars he's not up there more than ten minutes,' said the first. They all laughed.

'Done!' they all called and dollar bills appeared like magic in the middle of the wooden table. It was a diversion for men used to living dangerously who were now kicking their heels in this miserable sanctuary of a town with the blessing of Hank Whittle, saviour and tyrant.

They continued their game, but their attention was on the clock, the closed door above and the neat pile of dollar bills.

'He's taking his goddamned time,' one of them exploded.

'Well, you sure lost your bet,' someone remarked to the man at his side. 'Your ten minutes is up. I bet twenty and he's still at it.'

'Well, let's hope he'll stick it for an hour,'

laughed the man with the big cigar. The others looked both hopeful and disgruntled. 'But let's get on with this here game, or are you all upset because you might lose your bets?'

Sabre sipped his drink and leaned back against Rosie's pillows, his boots raking her not-so-clean bedcover.

He was relaxed, not fazed that he was in a whore's bedroom and that all the world knew it.

She stood before him hopefully, fingers hovering over the buttons on her bodice.

'Before we talk, wouldn't you. . . ?'

He shook his head. 'I'm sorry, Lovie. This is a business call. I want to talk about the outfit over the Bar Ridge.'

'Bar Ridge?' She tried to look puzzled.

'Come off it, Lovie, old girl. You know all about Holy Joe Stavinsky and his mob. God knows, his men must keep this crap hole in business. For a start, who works for who? Is it Holy Joe working for Hank Whittle or is it the other way around?'

'I don't know what you're talking about!'

'Then you're not as smart as I think you are.'

'What's it to you, anyway? Are you wanting to join them? If you do, you've gone the wrong way about it. Big Barney's a bad man to cross and Holy Joe sets much store by what Big Barney thinks and does.'

'Ah, so you do know something!' As he spoke, he casually drew a roll of bills from his vest pocket. Her eyes latched on to them greedily. 'Come on,

Lovie, tell me what you know. I can afford to be generous.'

She frowned. 'If you're not figuring to join the roost, just what are you up to? You're not aiming to kill off Holy Joe and take over the whole shebang? If you've got that into your head, forget it. He's got more guards than Fort Laramie.'

Sabre laughed. 'Nope! I've got me a tight little band whom I can trust. We travel light and fast. We can make a hit and run before the lawmen know we've struck. That's our secret, Lovie. No baggage to hold us back.'

'What about the woman?' Rosie asked jealously. 'Isn't she a drag?'

'Nope! As far as we're concerned, she's another man.'

'She doesn't think she is. I saw it in her face. She wants to be your woman, Sabre Wilde.'

'Goddammit! Is that all you women think about? You're talking foolish and she's just a kid. Now, about Holy Joe and Hank Whittle. Who runs whom?'

Rosie pursed her lips and thought awhile. Then she nodded slowly as if coming to a conclusion.

'You know I never gave it much thought, but now you mention it I think there's a tie-up. They could be partners. Holy Joe's boys come and go and there's trail herds coming in and out at various times. There's others coming in, too. Strangers, who only stay a while and move on, like messengers and such.'

'Messengers? What makes you think that?'

'Well, they talk funny. They come here, drink on the house and they make up to the girls and then they're gone.'

'They wouldn't be Russians?'

Rosie eyed Sabre sharply. 'We had a Russian drinking here a few days ago. Wounded he was, but he stayed long enough to get patched up and then he went off with Hank and I never saw him again.'

'Was his name Zaracov?'

'I don't know. I never heard it. But I did hear him ask about Holy Joe and where could he find him. I never saw him after that.'

Sabre nodded. 'Would you say the other strangers were Russian?'

She shrugged. 'Could have been. Funny accents, and one or two of 'em didn't know much English at all.'

'When will Holy Joe be back in town?'

'When he and the boys feel frisky.' She grinned. 'It's a high old time when they hit town. They're queueing three deep for our favours. That's when those who want to get out of this dump really get a good stake! What they don't give us we take when the drunken sots lie helpless on our beds!'

'Why don't you get out, Lovie?'

She grimaced. 'Where else could I go? Look at me, fat and showing wrinkles in the daylight. Where else could I pick up such easy cash?' She laughed harshly and poured herself another drink. 'Someday I will. I'll shock 'em all. I'll take what I've got in my little black stocking and go back East and get me a genteel cathouse where I can sit at the door and take the cash and offer the best girls that money can buy!'

For a moment she looked dreamy. Then she sighed.

'I don't think it will ever happen, but I can dream.'

'It could happen now, Lovie, if you wanted it. I could make it happen for you.'

Her eyes slitted as she watched his face.

'You're joking, aren't you? It's the first time I've heard that line. Why would you make it happen for me?'

'You help me; I help you.'

'How?'

'I want a man called Zaracov. It's personal and nothing to do with Holy Joe. I want to know if he's still at Bar Ridge. And I want him here in Baldarosa.'

She frowned, trying hard to remember. There was a stranger with Holy Joe the last time they had all hit town. Her memory was a little hazy. They all drank too much when Holy Joe met up with the boss, Hank Whittle, and the nights turned into orgies.

'Was he tall and dark, a bit of a charmer with a funny accent and good with the cards?'

'Yes, you might describe him so.'

'I don't know about the name,' she began doubtfully. 'Joe called him Ivan or something like that. I saw him at the tables. He wasn't interested in me, he likes young girls.'

'I believe so,' Sabre said gravely, thinking about Carla.

'What do you want him for?' Rosie's tone was sharp. She'd just remembered something that young Katie'd confided to her after they'd all ridden out of town.

'That's none of your business.'

Rosie took a deep breath.

'Katie said he was a killer. He knocked her about and laughed when he twisted her arm up her back.'

'Sounds like him. Did she say why he did it? Did he catch her riffling through his pockets?'

'No, Katie isn't like that. Far too frightened of what might happen to her. She said they'd rolled about the bed . . . you know how it is . . . when he grabbed her shoulders and twisted her around and shoved her arm up her back. She squealed and he laughed as if he got an extra thrill from her pain as he spent himself. She swears she'd never go with him again even if he offered her a goldmine.'

'Sounds like the bastard I'm after. You'll help me?'

'If it's the same feller, I'll help you for Katie's sake. She still hasn't got over the bruising she got from him. Me and the other girls are keeping Hank Whittle off her back. We're paying her dues for her.'

'Right. I want you to make sure he stays in the saloon.'

'That's no problem. He plays cards until midnight. It's only after that he wants a woman.'

'And tell the girls to get to their rooms by midnight. I don't want any accidents.'

She grinned. 'That's no problem either. They're all busy by then. Believe me, mister, it's a quick bang and on to the next one! There's a hell of a lot to service on Saturday nights!'

Sabre grinned. 'I bet half of 'em are sloshed out of their minds and won't know whether they've been with a woman or not.'

She gave a grin and a wink. 'That's when we get our own back. When they find they're skint, they make out they've had a good time. Nobody ever confesses to that kind of failure.'

They both laughed and Rosie poured more drinks. She had the feeling Sabre was loosening up. Maybe another drink or two and she would appear young and desirable once again. She leaned over him to give him his drink, making sure that he could get a good eyeful of what lay under her bodice.

He looked and his eyebrows lifted as he raised his glass.

'A toast, Lovie. I get what I want and you get what you want!' Their glasses touched and they were laughing when the door burst open, and Carla was there, glaring at them both. They froze.

'You lying bastard, Sabre Wilde! If you wanted

a woman why choose that dirty old cow?'

She crossed the room in a flash and, as Sabre rose from the bed, flung herself at him, fists pummelling his chest. He sank down upon Rosie's lacy pillows, cursing and dodging the blows. Carla was thin and wiry and she sure packed a punch.

Then she was being hurled aside by Rosie, whose temper was redhot and whose eyes sparked like fireballs.

'A dirty old cow, am I? I'll teach you, you scrawny little bitch!' she screamed, as she wound her fingers in Carla's long hair and dragged her around and then flung her through the door on to the landing where she sprawled half winded.

Rosie followed and lashed out with her foot at Carla's ribs.

'You bitch! I'll break every bone in your rotten little body. No wonder he doesn't want you,' she panted, as she tried another swipe at Carla's squirming body. 'You've no tits. You're all bone. He'd crack his nuts. . . .'

Sabre, both furious at Carla's onslaught and alarmed at Rosie's fury tried to intervene. He got a slap from Rosie and a kick on the shin from Carla's thrashing legs.

'You keep out of this!' snapped Rosie. 'Nobody, but nobody insults me to my face and gets away with it!'

But Carla was up and coming, fingers turned into claws as she raked Rosie's cheek and they closed together, two spitting wildcats rolling over and over and finally bumping and twisting as they fought their way down the stairs into the saloon.

The men in the bar watched avidly. There were whistles and catcalls and bets were taken on the merits of Rosie's experience in fighting and Carla's youth and suppleness.

'Five to two on Rosie,' bawled Hank Whittle, who'd seen Rosie in action many times before. 'Come on, you fellers. Make way for the ladies. This is better than betting on beetles!'

Hands waved in the air as some of the watchers assessed Rosie as a sure winner.

But there were others who fancied Carla's chances. Rosie was already bloodied, her bodice torn and two once-pert bosoms were on show for the pleasure of the gawkers. She was gasping and breathing heavily now, while Carla seemed to have got her second wind.

Carla had the strength of her anger behind her. Her head was on fire and she hurt badly inside because she imagined Sabre's rejection of her was because of her lack of femininity. Rosie's taunts infuriated her further. She wanted to kill the cruddy over-ripe whore.

Then suddenly strong hands were holding her, kicking and shouting, and a slap on the face shocked her into looking at her tormentor. It was Lucas and he was angry.

'Another squawk out of you and I'll tan your ass myself!' he yelled at her.

Confused, she looked across at Rosie who was being held by Sabre and looked mad enough to kick hell out of him if she could get to him. Carla's fury erupted again. Why couldn't it have been Sabre who held her?

She lunged away from Lucas who tripped her up and caught her as she sprawled on the floor. Now there was silence in the saloon. All those watching were curious as to what would happen next.

Then, awed, they watched Lucas pick Carla up and settle himself on a chair with her hanging over his lap. They counted aloud the strokes as he slammed his open palm down on her wriggling backside.

'One . . . two . . . three . . .' The counting got louder and louder and muffled Carla's shrieks.

Then when Sabre thought enough was enough, he caught Lucas's wrist in mid air.

'That's enough, Lucas. You're getting carried away,' he said between set teeth.

'She deserves it!' Lucas panted. 'She's like a bitch on heat where you're concerned.' Carla dropped to the floor where she lay and cried until Sabre hauled her to her feet and pushed her towards the batwing doors.

'Now git! And stop making a fool of yourself. If ever you pull a trick like that again, you're out, no matter where we are, you'll be out on your own. Get me?'

She nodded because she couldn't speak. Her

rear was on fire far worse than when she had blisters. She stumbled through the batwings to the
raucous laughter of the onlookers who now had
the job of deciding who was the winner on points.

NINE

'Come on, Carla, stop sulking. It's been two days now and Ma Gibbs says you've only come out of your room to go to the privy. It's Saturday night, so come out with Ned and me for a drink.' Bill Roscoe's voice through the door was wheedling, pleading.

'Go to hell! I hate this place! I wish I'd never heard of Baldarosa!'

Roscoe's voice hardened. 'You stupid little bitch! You'll have to come out sometime! You can't rot in there forever, unless you've got a yellow streak!'

'If you're trying to make me mad, then you'll be pleased to know you've done it, but I'm not coming out!'

'How's your ass?'

'Still painful and it's all black and yellow. I hate that Lucas. I could kill him!'

'Aw, come on now, you know you don't mean that. You were making a fool of yourself. . . .' He heard her sob. Poor kid. She was all mixed up. He

sighed. Maybe they'd been wrong to let her ride
with them. He could understand her not wanting
to face the ridicule of the town or confront Rosie
Lovett. Women could be so goddamn bitchy to
each other.

'Look, Ned's getting impatient. Are you coming
with us or not?'

'I've told you I'm not coming out. Isn't that
enough for you?'

He sighed. 'You can be stubborn, Carla. But
next time I come, I'll break the door down if you
don't come out. I promise.'

'Oh, go to hell,' she shouted wearily. 'Just leave
me alone!'

She heard him go down the wooden stairs and
turned her face into the hard pillow and allowed
herself the luxury of weeping. It wasn't often she
gave in to feminine weakness. She'd tried her best
to be one of the boys and not let Sabre down, but
sometimes it was all too much.

That was how she'd come to snap when she
knew Sabre had lied to her about that old cow.
How he could be interested in a raddled, over-fat,
over-painted lump of flesh, she couldn't understand. She cried until there were no more tears to
shed.

It was growing dusk when she finally got off the
bed and stood at the tiny window listening to the
racket coming from the saloon. There seemed to
be more uproar than usual. Hank Whittle was
sure making a good profit that night.

Then her ears picked up the faint clip-clop of horses coming at a brisk trot into town. She angled herself to watch from the grimy window and soon she saw the mass of men spreading across the dirt road coming into town.

She tried to count them as they rode in, but they came in bunched together nose to tail. She estimated there must be at least thirty men and maybe more. So this must be the Holy Joe gang the boys had talked about.

Then she drew her breath sharply, for riding with Holy Joe at the head, was a figure she recognized. Zaracov! He was as she remembered, dark and sombre, and the very sight of him sent the same sensations through her as when he'd held her captive. She shivered, but she wasn't cold.

Then the anger and burning hate shot through her as she remembered her pa and ma. She couldn't hide away in this room when there was the opportunity to kill him. She made up her mind quickly and, unlocking her door, she ran downstairs shouting for Ma Gibbs.

The old woman looked at her in amazement.

'Lawks! What's got into you? You could never dress up like one of them gals! You're too stringy for one thing!'

Carla took her by the shoulders and shook her.

'You said you did some of their washing. Isn't there a gown here I could wear?'

'Well, there's one of Lily's. She's about your size, but she's got a lot more up front. You could try it, but I can't see it on you somehow.'

'Just get it, and I want some hot water.'

'You can carry that upstairs yourself. I'm not your maid!'

But an hour later, she sucked her teeth and gave a whistle when Carla came downstairs, washed, hair combed and puffed up and coiled on her head and wearing the green gown as if she was used to wearing one every day of her life.

'Cor! I hardly recognize you. Here, I'll lend you my best black shawl.' Her eyes raked her and then she frowned when she saw Carla's scuffed boots peeping out from under the skirt. 'I'll lend you my best shoes too. They used to be my going-to-church shoes but I never wear them nowadays.'

'Thank you.'

'What are you going to do now?'

'I'm going into that saloon and I'm going to kill a man!'

'God in Heaven! What are you talking about? The feller only paddled your ass!'

'It's not him. It's the man who rode in with Holy Joe. Didn't you see them ride by?'

'Yeh, but I took no heed. They come in every Saturday night and cause a ruckus, so I keeps my head down. I don't want to get caught in any cross-fire that might come my way. You're not really going to kill one of Holy Joe's friends?'

But Carla did not answer, she was tugging on the shoes. Then, feeling for her little derringer she'd slipped into the pocket of the voluminous skirt, she was ready to go, and no words of Ma Gibbs would deter her from her confrontation with Zaracov.

Johnny Eagle Eye perched high on a rock watching the back trail. He liked the silence and the wind blowing in his hair. He was loyal to the man who'd given him back his life, but he didn't need the company of other white men. He disapproved of their ways and their disregard for the fundamental laws of this wild land. They never communicated with their ancestors and if they did worship, it was to a strange god who breathed fire and vengeance. That and their liking for gold made them strange creatures to Johnny Eagle Eye.

Now he sat facing the east, at peace with himself. He'd just had a vision and it was good. It would take time to interpret it, but he had all night.

Then his keen eyes saw the small cloud of dust rising into the air. He knew it was a large number of men on the move. So Holy Joe and his men were coming in as expected.

He watched with interest as they passed and especially the man riding with the leader. He recognized him as the Russian who had violated the squaw, Carla. He frowned. But Joshua was on the lookout too. He did not mix with the white men in the town. He, too, felt like an outsider. He would surely warn the boss. He could safely sit and watch and absorb the wonders of the night. . . .

Sabre was sitting at a table shuffling cards when Holy Joe and the boys came in. The locals downed their drinks and quietly left the saloon to the newcomers. The barman, helped out by the girls, was hard pressed to pour the drinks. Whiskey bottles appeared on the bartop like magic and the contents poured down thirsty throats straight from the bottle.

Soon there was the smell of slopped beer and a rising odour of unwashed bodies. A man had to shout to make himself heard.

Sabre stared at the man he knew must be Holy Joe and went on shuffling.

'Care for a game?' His eyes took in Zaracov and the cocky young gunslinger beside Holy Joe whom he reckoned must be Holy Joe's *segundo*.

'Why not?' It was Zaracov who answered and pulled out a chair and sat down opposite Sabre. The other two did likewise.

Sabre looked round at them all.

'Should we cut to deal?'

'When we see the colour of your dough,' Holy Joe said softly. 'The Lord provideth!'

Sabre laughed. 'He sure does!' He produced a roll of greenbacks and placed them before him. 'Gentlemen, what stakes shall we play for?'

Lucas sat drinking in a corner, watchful and waiting for trouble. He saw Roscoe and young Skinner elbow their way to the bar and nodded when Roscoe caught his eye. They were both alert and waiting for trouble.

It would come. The men were drinking fast and furious and quarrelling over the women. The murmur of voices grew higher as the night wore on. There was a buzz behind the cacophony of sound made up of excitement and tension.

It was difficult to concentrate. Sabre watched the eyes of the man opposite as he manipulated the cards with professional skill. He saw no recognition in the eyes. To Zaracov he was a stranger. He waited. His time would come for he sensed instinctively that Zaracov was controlling the cards.

The cash in front of each man rose and fell, a little more to Holy Joe, a little less to himself, while Zaracov and the fourth man barely made a mark. It was as if Zaracov was easing the tension ready to make his play. . . .

But Zaracov was becoming careless too. Suddenly Sabre's eyes narrowed and he caught Zaracov by the wrist.

'Hold it, mister! That ace you've got up your sleeve!' Zaracov sprang to his feet yanking his wrist free and, as he did so, the card fluttered on to the table.

'Why you. . . .' Zaracov's fist lashed out at Sabre whose gun was already pointing at Zaracov's middle.

Holy Joe and the *segundo* also came up from

their chairs knocking them over in the rush.

'Hold it, fellers! Let's not get carried away!'

Sabre turned grim eyes on Holy Joe.

'You in this too? Making a play between you? You thought I was just another sucker, didn't you, with easy dough easy lost! I suppose this galoot is just a stooge too?' He turned his Colt onto the silent fourth man.

'Hey, mister, I only does as I'm told. Turn that gun away!'

Sabre saw movement out of the corner of his eye. It was Holy Joe reaching for his weapon.

'I wouldn't do that if I were you.' Holy Joe's eyes flickered as he raised his hands, palms outward.

'Now see here, feller, it's all been a mistake. . . .'

'Some mistake! I think I'm entitled to the take.' Sabre reached forward with one hand to gather the piles of notes together.

Then he froze as the gun jabbed him hard in the back.

'Not so fast, mister.' Out of the corner of his eye he saw Hank Whittle standing behind him.

Then everything happened at once. Lucas went into action as did Roscoe and Skinner. Sabre ducked as Whittle's gun exploded into the air behind him. Then he whipped around and caught the other man in the stomach with a head butt. The *segundo* collapsed with a bullet in the shoulder and Holy Joe was aiming at Lucas while Zaracov was trying to overturn the table and duck behind it.

Holy Joe's men were scattering. This was the boss's business. They figured on keeping their skins intact. Bullets were flying like hornets as Roscoe and Skinner stood back to back cutting a swathe through the panicking onlookers.

Sabre saw Zaracov crouching low, intent on reaching the batwings for a quick getaway. He hurled an oncoming cowboy out of his path and stumbled over another who was groaning and holding his bloodied face.

'Zaracov! I'm coming after you!'

Zaracov heard Sabre's stentorian roar and scrambled to get outside. He pushed through the batwings and straightened upwards gulping fresh air. He looked back and waited. He would get the scar-faced bastard as he came through the swinging doors.

But he stiffened and froze at the sound of a gun being cocked behind him. He slowly turned, hands raised, and his eyes bulged at the sight of the girl in the fancy green gown of a saloon whore who was glaring at him, a small derringer firmly aimed at his midriff.

'What the hell!' He gave a lopsided smile. 'You're making a mistake, miss. The feller you want is inside. I'm waiting for him to come out.'

'I'm making no mistake, Ivan Zaracov. Don't you recognize me?'

He licked his lips. To his knowledge he'd never seen her in his life. He shook his head and then jumped as the batwings crashed on their hinges and convulsively he sent a couple of shots into the wooden panels.

Then a voice coming from the end of the veranda froze his blood.

'Carla, don't do anything stupid. I want him alive!' The dark figure of Sabre Wilde stepped into the light. Zaracov took two steps backwards.

'You bastard! It was all a mistake! You heard Holy Joe. You can have all the take. You can also have what I've got in my pocket.' He made as if to reach for his roll of bills and then a madness came over him and he fired two shots in quick succession, but his gun was empty of bullets. The trigger clicked twice uselessly. He cursed and threw it away and lunged at Wilde.

They grappled and rolled, punching and gouging, Zaracov's body being tossed and battered against the veranda supports. But he came back, head shaking and caught Sabre a punishing blow in the ribs. They fought silently, only their grunts and the thud of falling bodies piercing the night air.

Carla stood poised, ready and waiting. Sabre wanted this man alive, but she wanted him dead.

Then, when both men were staggering and their breath was coming in great gasps, Sabre made a mighty effort and closed with the Russian, raised him off the ground and swung him round and crashed him up against a water butt.

He crumpled, his legs giving way and, as Sabre stood leaning over and supporting himself while he got his wind back, Carla darted forward and raised Zaracov's head.

'You don't remember me, Zaracov?'

The man slowly shook his head, his breath spent.

'The little girl you raped repeatedly after you murdered her pa and ma? The girl who got away?'

Slowly he looked up at her, studying her face and realization came to him.

'The little vixen. . . .' He shook his head incredulously. 'You've changed. . . .'

'Yes, that little girl was left behind months ago and now you're going to pay for what you did. For my pa and my ma and for me!'

'Carla, don't do it!' Sabre sprang at her. 'I want him alive. I want to take him back. . . .'

But Carla wasn't listening. The derringer took Zaracov in the throat and the tatty green gown was spattered with blood.

Lucas and the others had prevented the mob from leaving the saloon with their drawn guns. But now they came through the batwings at the double. Lucas took in the situation at a glance.

'We'd better get out of here!' he shouted to the others, his glance scarcely taking in Carla's strange attire, but noting the smoking pistol.

Carla was frozen, still looking down at Zaracov, her lips drawn back in a snarl of revenge.

Sabre slapped her cheek, rocking her back on her heels.

'You mad bitch! Don't you realize what you've

done? He was a lead to the Russian unrest!'

Carla's hand came up to her bruised cheek.

'To hell with that! He murdered my folks and I'm glad he's dead!' and she lashed out at Sabre.

There were a couple of gunshots as Roscoe and young Ned held back the men fighting to get through the batwings.

'Hurry,' bawled Roscoe, 'get the horses. We can't hold them forever!'

Sabre grabbed Carla who was suffering from reaction. Lucas had gone ahead and now came down the street on horseback leading the rest. Sabre flung Carla aboard. There was the sound of tearing cloth as he slapped the horse's rump.

'My clothes! What about my clothes?' she shouted, as the horse sprang to a gallop.

'Never mind your clothes, get riding for your life!'

They rode hard for the rest of the night until after dawn broke over the hills, with only a couple of breathers for the horses. It was during their first break that Sabre reached into his saddle-bag and found his poncho. He threw it to her and smiled briefly. She was nearly at breaking point, but his manner conveyed his trust in her to keep up with them. The knowledge gave her strength. She could carry on.

TEN

Joshua waited for the dawn breaking over the far hills. It had been a long night. Then he climbed up the escarpment, sweating and cursing the reclusive Johnny Eagle Eye for his aversion to white folk. He was a good scout and loyal to the boss, but he was one hell of a feller to understand. Joshua would never admit to himself that he feared the sullen Apache, but his own superstitious upbringing made it impossible for him to cross him. Yet he knew that Johnny would give his life for him or any man who had Sabre Wilde's loyalty.

He paused, gasping, and then put two fingers together and gave a low whistle. It was like the hooting of an owl. He waited and then smiled as an answering call came.

Then Johnny was standing beside him. There had been no warning, no breath of movement. He was startled as he always was when Johnny appeared. The Indian's eyes glinted, the only sign of amusement at Joshua's startled jump.

'Jeese, Johnny. I don't know how the hell you do it!'

'When I was a child and my belly was empty I had to creep up on whatever I could catch. It made you both swift and sure. It was only when I became a dog soldier I grew proficient with a bow. It was part of the discipline for a boy hunter to glide through the forest like a snake! What is it you want?'

'They're coming and they're in a hurry. If we cut across country we can catch them along the trail.'

'Good. It is time to get the white man stink out of our nostrils.'

'The girl now ... I'm wondering about her.' Joshua spoke as they made their way to their horses.

'What about her? Wasn't she with them?'

'Yes, but she looked different. If I hadn't seen it for myself, I would never have believed it!' He shook his head disbelievingly. The Apache waited, knowing full well that Joshua wanted him to ask more questions. He flung a leg over his pony and waited. Joshua looked at him and grinned.

'You're a queer cuss! Aren't you curious?'

'Why should I be? Obviously you are going to tell me.'

'Well, believe it or not, she was wearing one of those low-cut gowns whores wear and I could see one of her goddamn legs as she rode as if the Devil was after her.'

'Maybe he was. It sounds as if they're expecting

trouble. We'd better get riding.'

They kept to the high ground, the upper track dipping and weaving, gradually working their way downwards towards the plain below. They could see stretches of the winding trail and got several glimpses of the bunched riders looking like moving dots far below.

They could calculate where the upper track joined the lower. They would be waiting, horses rested, well before the others showed up.

Then Johnny pulled on his pony's reins, muttering Apache cuss words that Joshua recognized.

'What is it, Johnny?'

The Apache didn't answer, but pointed far below. When Joshua screwed up his eyes he could see the cloud of dust coming along the trail. Johnny's keen sight had seen what he could not.

'Hell! Who might they be, Johnny?'

The Indian shrugged. 'Whoever they are, they're heading for Baldarosa, so my guess is they're owlhoot. We'll take a closer look.'

Carefully they picked their way down the steep escarpment at an angle that would bring them above the winding trail. They waited behind a pinnacle of dull red granite that gave them a good view of the oncoming riders. At the rate they were moving they would meet Sabre and the boys in a couple of hours.

Then Johnny drew in his breath sharply.

'See the glint on the leader's shirt?' Joshua rubbed his eyes and peered into the heat-hazed atmosphere. For a moment he saw nothing unusual and then, as the leader twisted to wave to his men, he saw the glint of the sun on what could only be a tin star.

'Jeese! Are they mad? That's a posse down there! Surely they're not expecting to shoot up the town? I wonder who they're trailing?'

Johnny shook his head.

'I don't like it. There's not enough of them to take on the town. My guess is that they'll hole up and wait for whoever they're after.'

They looked at each other, both suddenly thinking the same thing.

'You don't suppose they're after us?'

Joshua rolled his eyes. 'It figures. We've caused plenty of mayhem in these parts. Maybe we should ride back and warn the boss. We can lay up and watch them ride by and see if they're on the prod.'

The Indian didn't answer, but forked his horse in one lithe bound and, jerking on the rawhide reins, turned his pony in the direction they'd come.

They spoke very little as they rode the upper trail. It was rough going and hard on the horses. The lower trail wound far below, a grey dusty ribbon that sometimes ran along a riverbank and, at other times, was hidden by stands of scrubby trees. But at no point were they far from the lower trail.

The sun was going down when they finally

spotted the riders they were looking for. They were camped in the shelter of some stunted oaks beside a small stream. The smoke from a small fire betrayed their location and Johnny, far above on the escarpment gave his usual signal. Lucas lifted his head when he heard the call of a mating owl.

Then he was on his feet, waving his battered stetson at the two small figures outlined above on the ridge, relief at seeing the two men.

'They're up there, boss,' he shouted to Sabre, who was cleaning his horse's hooves in the stream-bed. Then he gave an answering call and watched the two men pick their way slowly down the escarpment leading their horses by the reins.

Sabre went to meet them. His face was grave when he returned with them. They all gathered round to listen.

'We've got to move, pronto!' Sabre said grimly. 'Get that fire out and be ready to ride in fifteen minutes.'

'What is it, boss? Is Holy Joe heading us off?'

'No. There's a posse coming up the trail. They should be here anytime as from now. We'll take to the rocks and watch and wait. They could be after us.'

He spoke quietly and calmly, all the time moving and packing up. Carla groaned.

'Hell! Why can't we stay here? They're probably not looking for us. They could be after anyone in that town!'

'Use your head, Carla. Sheriffs don't ride into towns like Baldarosa. They'd be sitting targets if they did. No, they're out looking for someone who's passed this way recently and, as far as I'm aware, we're the only outfit to come along this trail for days. They're trailing us, Carla, and if they think we're still in town, they're going to wait until we leave and catch us unawares. That's what I would do if I was heading that posse.'

'So we sneak away. Is that it?' Lucas looked angry.

'Yes, why not? We can't afford to be taken by any sheriff. Our cover could be blown and we can't allow that. Get moving! We haven't much time!'

'God damn it! How long do we have to live this hole-and-corner life?' Lucas sounded bitter. Of them all, he was the one who missed his family most and the good life he'd been used to. He missed the comfort and the gentility of young ladies and the social observances. The face of the woman he'd loved was blurred, and no longer stirred him, but he was still homesick for all the things he had now lost. He knew, like the others, that they were outcasts and there would be no going back.

'You knew how it would be, Lucas,' Sabre's voice broke in harshly. 'We're committed and it's our duty not to get caught!'

Roscoe and young Ned helped Carla and soon they were all moving out. There was no trace of fire or ash, Johnny had seen to that, and he followed behind the little cavalcade, brushing the ground behind them with a long leafy branch to obliterate their tracks.

They were none too soon. Far below them they could see the oncoming cavalcade. Sabre, curious as to the nature of the posse, took his binoculars and watched the oncoming men, concentrating on their leader. Lucas watched beside him. Then Sabre shook his head and offered the glasses to him.

'Take a look, Lucas. See if you recognize anyone.'

But Lucas drew a blank.

'Maybe they're not after us, boss. Maybe they're just running into trouble without realizing it.'

'No. No posse in the world would ride into Baldarosa without knowing what they're up against.'

'Not unless the posse's a phoney, or the sheriff's mixed up with Holy Joe and his outfit!'

They stared at each other.

'The sonofabitch! That figures. Holy Joe must have friends in high places to run a spread on those lines. It would take the army to shift him. Now I wonder. . . .' Sabre looked pensive. 'I wonder how far off we are from the nearest tele-graph wires?'

Johnny, who'd been standing with folded arms and that inscrutable look on his face which Ned Skinner detested, spoke, pointing to the east.

'One day's ride. The singing wires stretch from east to west.'

'I think we'll hole up, boys, and I'll take a ride. I've got to check with Washington about the Zaracov affair. I can make some enquiries about Joe Stavinsky. He maybe ties in with the unrest up in Alaska.'

'I go back to Baldarosa and watch,' Johnny said solemnly. 'I watch and maybe see this Holy Joe meet with this tin star stranger. They not recognize me for not being in town.'

Sabre nodded. 'You take Joshua with you?'

'No. He get in the way. He stand out too much among Indians. I go alone and only have me to worry about!'

'Why you ornery son of a bitch!' Joshua said hotly. 'When did you ever worry about me? I can look after myself!' Johnny gave one of his rare smiles.

'All the time I worry about you! You are my buddy. I want you in one piece, not full of holes!'

'Gee, Johnny, I didn't know you cared!' but Johnny missed the sarcasm in Joshua's voice.

'I care for all of you. You are my family. We are blood brothers. Now I go, before we become spineless squaws!'

He slipped away without a backward glance. Joshua watched him go, a wide grin on his shiny black face.

'I'll be damned! He was nearly human!' He shook his head. 'I'll never understand that ornery son of a gun!'

'Why bother to try?' Roscoe exclaimed. 'He's

loyal and trusty and would give his life for the boss. Believe me, I'd rather have him on our side than against us!'

They were all quiet as they made camp, especially Carla.

'You think he'll be all right?' she asked Roscoe, as they ate their meal.

'Yeh, sure. He's a wily bird, is Johnny.'

'I'm a bit frightened of him, but I feel safer when he's around. Sounds funny, doesn't it? I've never known an Apache before, but he seems part of this wilderness. He doesn't see his surroundings like we do.'

'I know what you mean, girl. Johnny's an extension of the forest. He interprets things differently to what we do. We're the strangers and the despoilers. He's one of the guardians. It's the way he sees Nature as being God. That's why he doesn't mix with us. He's with us but not of us. See what I mean?'

She nodded slowly.

'I'm beginning to. It must have been dreadful when he was drummed out of his tribe for killing his wife and his brother. His whole way of life changed forever.'

'Yeh, well, all of us have had our lives changed for better or worse. Best thing, girl, is to take each day as it comes.'

They were all bedded down for the night when Sabre quietly saddled up his horse and headed east to find the singing wires.

*

Mal Buchan and his men made good time and reached Baldarosa just before dusk. They tied their sweating horses to the hitching rail in front of The Baldarosa Belle and Buchan tossed a quarter to a lounging half-breed who caught it in a grubby fist.

'Take the horses to the livery and get 'em fed and rubbed down. I'll pay you later.'

'Yes, sir!'

The town drunk watched the men mount the veranda steps with a rattle of spurs and enter eagerly. He could understand their hurry, his tongue licking dry lips as he thought of Hank Whittle's rotgut whiskey.

The horses with heads down, coats bathed in foam and sweat were no trouble. They sensed water and feed and followed the lumbering figure eagerly. Soon, Whiskey Will was helping the ostler in the comparative luxury of the stable. Many a night he'd lain alongside the stabled horses when he was drunk out of his mind. Now Greg Masters grinned at him.

'Got yourself a meal ticket, Will?'

'Maybe, maybe not,' growled Will.

'You buy yourself some grub and forget the whiskey, man. You're killing yourself.'

'What of it? It's my life!'

'Aw, come on, Will. You used to be a regular wizard with horses! You and me could have made real dough. Me tending them and you shoeing 'em. Why don't you get wise to yourself?'

Whiskey Will shrugged stooped shoulders.

'I don't shoe horses no more. They don't trust me. Look at my hands. He held out gnarled fingers that trembled.

'Shucks! That's the whiskey, Will.'

'Nah! I've lost my nerve! I'm shot to hell!' and he kept mumbling as he brushed down one of the horses with a handful of hay. Greg Masters shook his head and went to fetch a measure of corn for each horse.

Mal Buchan and his men crowded around the bar, all bellowing for service and soon Rosie and the girls were there, teasing and tempting. But at the moment all they wanted was to quench their thirst.

Mal Buchan looked around for Hank Whittle.

'Where's the boss?' The barman didn't answer, but jerked a thumb towards the back room.

'Got a private card game going, has he?'

The man nodded. 'Private, very private.'

'Got something else going, eh?'

The barman gave him a look of suspicion and slapped down a glass and a bottle in front of him. He glared at the pin mark on Mal Buchan's vest where a tin star might have been.

'It don't do to ask questions around here, mister.' Then he stomped off to the other end of the bar to serve the clamouring men.

Mal Buchan poured a shot and drank while his
eyes wandered around assessing the local
drinkers. They were a cutthroat lot and he was
glad he knew Hank Whittle. Then he was startled
by low feminine laughter and a hand resting
seductively on his shoulder. He smelled cheap
perfume.

'Hya, stranger! What about buying me a drink?'
and he was looking into Rosie's laughing eyes.

He surveyed her and was not impressed. Too
old, too fat, too experienced. But she could be
useful.

He bowed gallantly.

'Of course. Be my guest.'

Rosie bawled to the barman, 'Sam, another
glass down here.' Sam slid a glass along the bar
with the ease of much practice. She poured a
generous shot and raised the glass to Mal.

'Here's to whatever you're looking for! I'm
Rosie, usually called Lovie by my friends. Who are
you?'

'Mal Buchan, and looking for Hank Whittle.'

She raised her eyebrows. 'A friend of Hank's? I
never heard him speak of you.'

'We go back a long way.'

She put her head on one side and looked at him
mischievously.

'How about you and me taking this here bottle
and going upstairs and having . . . er . . . a little
chat? I could help you. You see, Hank's mighty
choosy about who he sees these days.'

Her hand slipped down his shoulder and a fingernail scraped at his vest where the tin star had been.

'Seems mighty strange, Mal Buchan, you got all the hallmarks of a sheriff!' She smiled secretively. 'What about our little chat?'

Mal Buchan cursed inwardly. God damn her eye! He knew he had to walk a thin line. One scream from her and guns would spit before a question was asked.

'We can chat here,' he said easily, and turned and leaned against the bar. As he did so he reached for his roll and quietly peeled off several greenbacks. 'Here, I think this takes care of our little chat.' Her hand came out like a snake and the notes were stuffed down the front of her bodice. 'How do I get to see Hank Whittle?'

'Through that door.' She pointed to the door behind the bar. 'But at the moment there's a private party going on and anyone opening that door before he rings for Sam, is likely to get a dose of buckshot. I wouldn't risk it, Mal Buchan.'

'Who's with him?'

'Oh, the big shots of the town, including Holy Joe Stavinsky. They play for big stakes. You know how it is. They're all holed up and bored out of their minds. Gambling and whoring and drinking are the only things they do around here.' She laughed bitterly. 'We had a diversion a little while back. The Wilde bunch rode in, but they didn't stay. Shot the place up and scarpered and our boys were too drunk to do anything else but chase 'em out of town. A pity. A good hanging would have made a change.'

Mal Buchan cursed and poured another drink and swigged it down in one gulp.

'Hell! We've just missed the bastards!' He cursed again. Rosie looked at him curiously.

'What you want Sabre Wilde for? There was a woman with him, was she yours?'

'A woman? Nah, never heard of her. I want him and I'll get him if I have to follow him to the ends of the earth.'

'What's he done to you?'

'He killed my brother.'

Just then the door behind the bar opened and Hank Whittle followed by Holy Joe and the other gamblers came out. Whittle looked pleased while Holy Joe looked a little disgruntled.

'Better luck next time, Joe. There's always another time.'

'I don't know how you do it,' Holy Joe spat, 'but when I do, you're gonna pay!' He joined some of his boys.

Hank looked at Rosie and Mal. He frowned and then smiled.

'Mal Buchan! How many years is it, buddy?' He put out a hand to him. 'I hope Rosie's looking after you real good! Sam, a bottle of the best stuff. Come in here and we'll have a jaw.'

The room was hazy with smoke from the gamblers and smelled of stale beer and sweat.

Hank indicated a chair and Mal sat down.

'Now Mal, what brings you to these parts?'

'I'm hunting Sabre Wilde. He killed my brother John.'

'The bastard was in here earlier.' He turned and bawled at Holy Joe, 'Get over here, Joe. There's someone here hunting the feller who started the ruckus when that Russian of yours got shot by that little whore.'

Holy Joe's eyes glittered as he came to join them.

'I'd like to get that cuss and the girl. They stymied a deal I had with Zaracov, God rot them!'

Mal Buchan eyed him up, not liking the look of the tall, cadaverous figure dressed in black frock-coat and tight buckskins. He reminded him of a hellfire preacher or, worse, an undertaker. He had a bad feeling about him, but he let none of his thoughts show in his face.

'What say we get together and go after the bastards? There's only a handful of them. We could muster up fifty men between us.'

Holy Joe laughed.

'We could have us a ball with those odds. "Vengeance is mine, sayeth the Lord". We could do His work and string up the sinners so that they be a warning to others who become too jumped up for their station!' Holy Joe actually glowed with enthusiasm. Mal Buchan looked at Hank Whittle in amazement. This feller was a nut. He should have been in a pulpit pounding out hellfire and damnation, not running a crooked outfit in the wilderness.

'Yeh, well, I'd settle for a quick, sharp shootout and be done with it,' he muttered.

'We'll take them alive, and we'll make 'em suffer, to redeem their souls and purify them before they meet their Maker,' Holy Joe intoned.

'Yeh, well, whatever you want, mister, as long as they're stiffed at the end of it!'

The sun was high when Sabre Wilde drew up in camp. His shoulders sagged and there was a film of dust over both him and his horse. He had ridden hard all through the night to locate the telegraph wires which now stretched east to west and north to south following rail tracks and connecting cities and towns that were springing up all over the West.

The news he brought back was breathtaking. Zaracov had been a major dissident in the unrest up in Alaska and Joseph Stavinsky was a wanted man. He was a known agitator, a fire-eater, who masked his real goals of organizing a new power struggle by spouting the gospel to ignorant rebels.

Sabre looked around the listening group, his face drawn and tired.

'You know what it means?'

Roscoe spat into the fire. 'Seek out and kill!'

Lucas turned away without a word and went to pack. Carla looked from one to another.

'Does that mean we're going back?'

'Not necessarily you, Carla. These are our orders, not yours or Joshua's. You both can stay here and look after the camp.'

Carla's eyes flashed.

'I'm one of you, remember? Where you go, I go. I'll get ready.'

Sabre turned to Joshua who grinned. 'Count me in, boss. I'm hurt you'd think otherwise. Besides, someone's got to look after the Indian!'

Lucas returned. He'd unpacked the ammunition and also carried a couple of bundles of dynamite.

'I think, boss, if we're to do the job right, we should clear out the vipers' nest. What d'you think?'

'What about the womenfolk?'

'No problem. Surprise the bastards and while they're panicking, we'll hustle the women out.'

'You're the ladies' man. I'll leave you to figure on how to do it.'

Lucas grinned. 'This is when Carla will come in useful. She'll get to them easier than any of us.'

'Well? What are we waiting for? Let's ride!'

Night had fallen when they arrived on the outskirts of Baldarosa. The town was alive with newcomers. Holy Joe had sent for all his men and now they were making the most of their visit to town.

Joe Stavinsky cursed long and fluently. They were out of control, all hard-bitten men, who seized every chance to indulge their physical passions. There was a carnival atmosphere. Tonight they would drink and fornicate. Tomorrow they would go on the manhunt.

Sabre and Lucas watched the revelry from high ground. Somewhere out yonder were Joshua and the Apache who were to make a diversion by firing the livery stable and letting loose the horses from the corral. Young Ned was close by. His orders were to follow Sabre when Lucas left with Carla to see to the womenfolk. Ned was carrying the dynamite in a leather bag that hung from his neck. He also wore a bandoleer packed with extra bullets. He was trembling with excitement. He usually rode with Roscoe. Now he was marking the boss while Roscoe tucked himself away with his high-powered rifle trained on the batwings of The Baldarosa Belle.

Suddenly there was a roar from the men below.

'Fire!' someone called, and many voices took up the cry.

'There we go!' shouted Sabre. 'Good luck, Lucas, and watch the girl!' Lucas was away and Sabre waved to Ned and took the first stick of dynamite, lit it and counted to three, then threw it in a wide arc down, down, down, until it alighted directly in front of Hank Whittle's store and went up in a whoosh that lit up the sky.

Then Sabre was scrambling to another site and again threw a smouldering stick down amongst the wooden shacks that made up the town.

There was a surge of men fighting to get out of the saloon. There were shouts and screams as the men came out and looked wildly around, thinking they were surrounded by the army.

Sabre heard the high-pitched whine of Roscoe's rifle in rapid succession as he scrambled from one vantage point to another. He wondered about Lucas and the girl, and how Johnny and the black man were doing.

'Ned, give me the rest of the dynamite and make your way to where Lucas and the women will make for. Look after them and tell Lucas to keep back from the saloon. I'm going to blow it in fifteen minutes.'

'Yes sir!' and Ned was away, crouching low.

Then Sabre made his way down towards the saloon. There was no sign of Hank Whittle or Joe Stavinsky. Roscoe had orders to shoot either of them. Maybe it would take dynamite to force them out.

The crowd were milling around, letting off their guns and fighting each other with the mistaken idea that Holy Joe's outfit was there to take over the town.

Sabre heard Roscoe's trained salvo of bullets and threw two sticks with seconds between, and then he was running, crouched low and into the saloon and just in time to hear Hank Whittle screaming at Holy Joe.

'You did this, Joe Stavinsky. You set us up and now you're paying for it, you son of a bitch!'

Then everything seemed to happen at once. Sabre's arm came up and the smoking stick of dynamite rolled over the floor as Whittle's gun exploded harmlessly into the air as his eyes took in the sizzling explosive. Holy Joe's gun left its holster, but one look and Holy Joe dived through the window, shattering shards of glass and cutting himself in the process.

Mal Buchan, who'd had his back to the batwings whirled about, saw the smoking missile and dived for the door and landed in a roll outside following Sabre Wilde. With a yell that could be heard above the cacophony of sound, Mal made a grab for Wilde and missed and went down from Sabre's kick to the groin.

Then Sabre was running madly for cover noting as he did so, the whine of a high-powered rifle bullet. Out of the corner of his eye, he saw Hank Whittle slam back against the swinging batwing doors just as the saloon exploded into an orange fireball spitting out heat and debris. Then came the horrendous crackle of burning wood and the angry pop of exploding bottles and kegs.

Sabre Wilde took a deep choking breath. Good old Roscoe. He'd got Whittle, but where the hell was Joe Stavinsky?

Staggering away from the blazing heat, he made for the empty corral at the back of the fiercely burning building. Smoke was enveloping the entire area and his eyes smarted. It was like drowning in a sea of cotton wool. He coughed and, as he did so, he heard an answering cough and made for the horse trough in the corner of the corral.

It was then two figures rose from the murk and stench and closed with him. Two fists like shovels clamped about his neck from behind while he took a head butt to his stomach. Hands frantically trying to unloosen the stranglehold, he saw the charging figure and braced himself and at the same time brought up his knee and caught his assailant in the groin. There was a gasping scream as the man fell away and Sabre summoned up all his strength to heave the man behind him over his shoulders.

The man screamed as his hands loosened and he fell to the ground with arms and legs splayed like a rag doll. Sabre bent forward to take several ragged breaths and saw Johnny loom out of the smoky haze, reach down and pull his knife out of the man's back. He took the man by the hair and raised him up.

'Is this the man you were ordered to seek out and kill?'

Sabre staggered over and looked at him, his chest and throat raw, his voice a croak.

'Yes, that's him, Johnny, that's Joe Stavinsky, wanted for murder and crimes against the United States of America.'

'Do you want him scalped, boss, as a means of identification?'

'No, Johnny. Search him. We'll send anything

we find back to Washington. They can deal with it there.'

Sabre turned to look for his other attacker, but he was gone. He figured it was the lawman. Well, at least Stavinsky was accounted for.

Mustering his strength, he turned back to monitor the fighting that was still going on between the townsfolk and Joe Stavinsky's men with the sheriff's posse fighting both sides. If Sabre hadn't been nearly all in he would have relished the joke.

It was then Big Mal Buchan pounced, catching Sabre Wilde a mighty swing to the jaw. Sabre saw it coming at the last moment and took the blow on the side of his neck. Sabre rolled away and, as Mal Buchan came at him again with lips drawn back in a wolfish grin, he bounded on to his feet and sidestepped as Mal's weight carried him forward. Sabre saw the knife in Mal's hand. So the bastard had lost his gun.

Then Sabre was ducking and weaving, conscious of the swish of the knife. He felt the sharp pain when it ripped his sleeve and drew blood, the warm stickiness seeping down on to his left hand.

He feinted to the left and caught the lawman on the nose drawing blood and feeling the mishmash of bone.

Then the big man put out a foot and Sabre tripped and fell headlong. Swiftly as a snake darting for the kill, he felt the weight of the other man punching the breath out of him.

Then came the silent struggle as Sabre's hand grasped the hand wielding the knife. Their clasped hands trembled between them, inches from their faces. Sabre smelled the fetid breath that pumped out from gaping jaws and heard the gasping words rung from the other man.

'This is for my brother, you murdering lump of shit! I hope you rot in Hell!'

'And who might he be?' panted Sabre, as he twisted and rolled, while striving to bring up his knee, the knife flashing between them.

'John Buchan. You shot him when he was in bed with a woman. You didn't give him a chance!'

For a moment, Sabre Wilde was off guard with surprise. So he'd been right. The posse had been trailing them, but for personal reasons, not because they were out to catch the Wilde boys.

Suddenly his grasp on the hand was gone and the knife came down in a vicious arc. He kicked violently, catching a shin bone and hearing it snap. The knife embedded itself in the ground near his shoulder. Then, as Mal Buchan struggled desperately to free the knife, Sabre twisted and grabbed the man's neck and heaved all his weight on it. Mal Buchan scrabbled at the ground, his eyes bulging, his tongue protruding while a choking gurgle came from tormented lungs.

Then came the sickening snap and the body sagged. Sabre rolled away and lay gasping and heaving.

It was Joshua who found him and hauled him upright.

'Boss, it's time to go. There's men out there itching for a lynching party. Lucas says we must git!'

Sabre nodded. It figured. They wouldn't be popular in these parts.

'What about Carla and the women?'

'Carla's fine. The woman called Rosie died in the fire. Stupid bitch went back for her stash. It was in a black stocking and she was caught in the blast. The others voted to go back and start again.'

'Poor Lovie. She wanted so much to get away. How are the others?'

'Ned got burnt trying to drag Rosie away. Lucas got a bullet in the arm, but Roscoe's OK.'

'And Johnny?'

'That son of a bitch must have had his spirits watching over him. He always said he could deflect slugs and arrows. I believe him!'

Sabre smiled as he followed Joshua to their rallying point. He grinned at them all as he joined them. The horses were ready. It was time to ride.

Carla came and put her arms about him and kissed him on the mouth.

'I'm glad you're safe.'

'Stop it! You're going all soft on me.'

'You look like death.'

'So would you if you'd ridden for twenty-four hours and then fought for your life.'

'What would we have done if you'd been killed?'

He shrugged. 'Lucas would carry on and take

orders from Washington. But don't you know I'm indestructible? I'm like Johnny here, I've got a guardian angel.'

She looked at him as if she half believed him.

'I don't know about you having a guardian angel, but I know you are mine.'

He laughed and kissed her which pleased her and then chucked her under the chin.

'Get your rump moving. We've a long way to go.'

Lucas looked at him enquiringly.

'Where do we go from here, boss?'

'First to report to Washington and then, who knows? We'll take a vote on it, unless Washington says otherwise.'

The little cavalcade of voluntary outcasts moved off, straight-backed and alert, unconsciously getting ready for their next assignment.